The Friar Cave Mysteries

Sylvia Bigit

CRIME SCENE

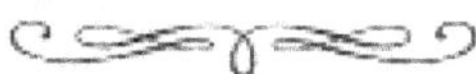

Nothing exciting ever happens on the island of Pasman—a tiny spec of land in the quiet and tranquil Adriatic Sea. At least that's what the teenagers of the island thought. That's why they couldn't wait to leave for the big cities on the mainland of Croatia, or in other countries, once they were ready to attend university. To pass the time of the never-ending teenage years, a few industrious kids found part time jobs at local hardware or grocery stores on the island, some farmed the family land, and some just became lazy. Some found ways to sneak liquor and cigarettes, while others hung out at local cafés shooting the breeze and did nothing much except sleep and eat and dream. But not sixteen-year-olds Milena and Rosana. They preferred to explore the dangerous, less traveled, and difficult to get to areas of the island, because they knew if something exciting ever were to happen on Pasman, that's probably where it would be.

It was a sunny and blustery late summer day as Milena and Rosana made their way along the sloped, but rocky mountain. They were pros at traversing this particular mountain with its rugged terrain as they had been coming up to this mountain since they were little girls. The rocks actually helped them in their walk to the top because they gave them a foothold and kept them from slipping backward. But it was a daring challenge today since there was nothing to obstruct the strong cold bura wind from knocking a person over. Walking up the mountain on such a day wasn't the smartest idea they've had, but they were teenagers and sometimes teenagers liked to challenge the elements as well as authority. So, they thought that since they were familiar with this mountain and proficient at navigating to the top, they could withstand the wind. They continued marching on despite the howling wind hammering their backs and slapping their clothing around like sails in a storm, while bracing themselves against the sporadic fierce gusts of wind. As they walked, they sometimes kept their hands tucked into their jacket pockets and other times they vigorously rubbed their arms over their middle sections in an attempt to keep some body warmth against the fierceness of the wind. They carried on even though it was getting harder and harder to keep their balance in order to avoid falling.

As they continued going further up the mountain, they heard several dogs barking. The path they took brought them directly through what used to be the main street of an ancient hamlet. It was more of a micro village as it only consisted of about a dozen dwellings. The buildings were very small and built from stones readily available on the rocky mountain. A few years ago, some of the dwellings had caved in roofs or had pieces of wall missing. But the current owner remodeled many of the houses. Now the village had a quaint, neat and beautifully restored original look that brought you back to ancient times. This place used to be the main village back in medieval times when the pirates raided the Adriatic Sea and villages. The hamlet was built half way up the mountain, with a clear view of the sea. The decision to build the houses half way up the mountain was intentional. It served to deter the pirates from raiding the hamlet and it provided the villagers ample time to sound the alarm of approaching pirate ships. This gave the residents time to band together and arm themselves in defense of an anticipated attack. Both girls loved that quaint little ancient hamlet, as it stirred their imagination with images of more exciting times in the days when pirates ruled the seas.

A wealthy but humble American single man, who cherished his privacy, now owned the ancient village. Some of the houses he renovated were used as his home, business, workshop, and barn for his animals. He also had an early warning alarm system … his large dogs! They started barking well before anyone even reached the compound. And though the girls always brought dog biscuits with them to give to the dogs, they barked relentlessly regardless of the biscuits. Milena was especially fond of a black and white spotted Dalmatian named Rocky. Whenever she came up the mountain, he greeted her with a wildly wagging tail that made his entire rear end move from side to side. She opened the chain link fence gate and threw some of the biscuits onto the ground for the dogs. But Rocky ignored the yummy offerings. Instead, he ran to Milena, sprung up on his hind legs and placed his front paws on her torso as if trying to give her a hug, and showered her face with dog kisses. The love affair between her and the dog was mutual. Once the greeting was over, she led him out of the fenced area and closed the gate behind her. She held a biscuit at her eye level and said, "Jump!" The dog obediently jumped and snatched the biscuit from her hand. Then she crouched down and rubbed his ears as he ate the biscuit.

"Yes, yes, I missed you too Rocky," she said in a baby like voice.

Rocky quickly devoured the biscuit and then resumed showering her face with slobbery wet kisses. It was a game they both loved to play.

Rosana, on the other hand, gravitated toward Butch, the Alpha German Shepard dog of the group. He was also Steve's main hunting dog. The other two large dogs, Cosmo and Smokey, were your run-of-mill mixed breed mutts.

As usual, Steve the owner, came out of one of the buildings to see what was going on.

"Oh, it's you two again," he said. "Don't you ever get tired of coming up here? And, Jesus, are you both crazy or what, coming up here during a bura?"

"Oh Steve, we just came up here to see if you were alright," teased Milena.

"Ha! Oh, I see," said Steve. "So now you girls are worried about MY wellbeing, huh?" he said laughing.

"We're going up to the cave," said Rosana smiling.

"Like I couldn't guess," said Steve sarcastically. "Well, I've gotta go feed the dogs. You girls be careful now. The gusts are pretty strong."

They assured him that they would be careful and proceeded on their way.

Steve was a tall man of just over six feet, and rather handsome. He looked to be in his forties with black hair, blue eyes, a suave complexion, and a beard that needed trimming. He was wearing his signature blue jeans and button down light blue shirt—which brought out the color of his eyes—tucked into his pants. He sometimes smoked a pipe which gave him an air of sophistication, something that was sorely lacking in the village below. He didn't mind the girls coming up to the compound as there were very few visitors that came up the mountain using this path. There was a drivable road a little further north of the village that people used to come up to the mountain, but that road did not go far enough to reach the cave, which was located in the midst of a forest and a mess of bramble. But that road did afford a great scenic view, so most people used it rather than the one that went past his compound. Steve had known the girls for about eight years and was well acquainted with each of their parents. He welcomed and enjoyed their company any time they came up his path. Even though Steve had no children of his own, he viewed the girls as his surrogate daughters.

Sometimes, in good weather, the girls would explore some of the other empty buildings in the village. Steve didn't mind. The girls loved to imagine what it must have been like to live there and have to navigate your way down the mountain every day to go plow a field or to harvest a crop down where the fields are fertile. That's where the current village was. Back in those days, though, they only had donkeys to help carry the load.

"How on earth did they get the plows down there?" asked Milena.

"They didn't have plows like we know them today, and they didn't have horses either," answered Rosana. "They used hand plows and hand tillers, which was exhausting work. Some of the old timers still do it the hard way. Didn't you notice some of the old huts at the foot of the mountain? That's where some of the farmers would spend the night if they were too tired to make the trip back up the mountain after plowing their fields all day. They would take water, bread, cheese and prosciutto with them just in case."

"Yes, I guess you're right, but I can't imagine doing hand plowing or tilling, especially if you're old," said Milena.

"Our people are resilient and strong well into their old age," said Rosana.

They both decided that it was a very hard life and were glad they didn't live up in the mountains. These days, all the picturesque villages were down by the sea on relatively flat and fertile land, so there was no need to go to the mountain except if you needed firewood, or wanted to pick some wild herbs that grew abundantly on the mountain.

As they looked down at the scene below them, they saw the normally tranquil Adriatic Sea, now violently angry due to the bura winds, crashing to the shore. Large white caps took the place of the normally quiet deep blue water. And when a wave hit the jetty at the beach, the wave and sea spray flew high into the sky and crashed over the jetty. Through the misty sea smoke, they saw the fishermen's boats bobbing up, down and side to side, tossed around like toy boats in a bathtub. The salt from the water permeated everything. The girls felt it in their nostrils and tasted it on their tongues. The sailors had a saying, "When the bura sails, you don't." The girls saw firsthand how true that was. Though they both had on jackets with a hooded sweat shirt underneath, it just wasn't enough to keep the wind from going right through them. When strong gusts of winds suddenly and wildly blew, it would catch the hood and rip it off their head leaving their hair to fly straight up into the air. And if they dared to turn their heads to the side against the wind, their eardrums felt like a hurricane was howling in their ear. So, they continued to tuck their chins into their jackets and hug their bodies with their elbows and arms while trying to shake off the cold.

The bura wind is an icy-cold, bone-chilling north or north-eastern wind that blows in strong gusts along the Adriatic Sea from the Dinaric Alps, and can make a warm sunny day feel as if you were in Siberia. Bura winds occur mostly in winter and it's not unusual for gusts to reach speeds of over 130 miles an hour on average. At this speed, if the winds were 130 miles per hour in the United States, it would be considered a category four hurricane. At times, the bura has been known to even throw fish out of the sea with its fierce waves, and overturn cars with its sheer power. Fortunately, the coastal homes of stone and concrete with their red clay tile roofs were built to withstand the wind's brutal force. There is also a bura wind that blows in the summer. It's not as fierce as the winter bura wind and it lasts for only about three days, but the gusts can be very strong.

Some of the farmers liked the bura wind and referred to it as "the good wind." As they often explained, "The wind not only clears the air and makes it crystal clear, but it also clears the mind and makes you feel refreshed and glad to be alive." On a clear day after the bura, the scene is very different. The deep blue sea sparkles like diamonds in the sunlight and the seaside houses with their red tile roofs are clearly visible nestled between the sea, the mountains and the sky. Looking into the distance one could see the Italian alps when standing on the mountain top. The villagers also appreciated the bura, as it is good for drying not only laundry on a clothes line, but also for drying prosciutto. In the coastal region of Croatia, known as Dalmatia, the reason the Dalmatian Prosciutto or Prosut (pro-shoot), as it's called on the Dalmatian coast, is so special is the way it's made. As with most foods in Croatia, they don't believe in using artificial preservatives or ingredients. It gets its delicious distinctive flavor because of the smoke that comes from a specific type of wood used in the smoking process and because of the drying effect the bura wind has on the prosut when it's hung to dry. There is a saying, "Without the bura, there is no good prosut."

The mountain cave intrigued both Milena and Rosana, and they came to the mountain to explore the cave frequently just to get away from the humdrum life of the world around them where, according to them, "nothing exciting ever happens." They imagined what it must have been like to be a pirate in ancient times with swashbuckling adventure at every port-of-call. As kids they would pretend to be pirates with a black patch over one eye, a scarf wrapped around their waist and a stick in their hand for a sword. A romantic notion of two unworldly young girls.

"You know, back in about the 200s BC, when Croatia, Bosnia/Herzegovina, Montenegro, and Albania were called Illyria, Queen Teuta, known as the Pirate Queen, allowed the Illyrian pirates to raid the merchant ships and shores, including Rome's. Their raids were so frequent that the sea wasn't even safe to travel anymore," said Rosana. "So, Rome sent two ambassadors to negotiate an end to the piracy, especially with regard to Rome's ships, but the Pirate Queen refused and told them piracy wasn't illegal. However, when one of the ambassadors was killed, Rome waged war against the Illyrians. Queen Teuta, with her pirates and powerful navy was one of the few truly powerful women in antiquity and she fought for all it was worth until 228 BC. Unfortunately, though, Rome's power was on the rise at the time, so the Pirate Queen was finally defeated."

"Sounds like my type of woman," said Milena. "How exciting it must have been in those days!"

Milena was a pretty girl of medium height and build with dark brown hair, blue eyes and a wicked sense of humor that always made Rosana laugh. That's what Rosana loved most about her best friend Milena, her ability to make her laugh. Besides her brown hair and blue eyes, Milena just had a way about her. The way she walked with confidence and purpose, the way she spoke with conviction and most of all, her beautiful contagious smile. She often acted silly, but she was smart and sexy and intimidated many of the boys in the village simply by walking into a room. Rosana was shorter and thinner than Milena with blonde hair and brown eyes. She, like her mother, was very adventurous and nothing stopped her from her next adventure. Besides being a beauty in her own right, Rosana was a very logical thinker and somewhat of a computer nerd, so she knew a little information about a lot of different things. Like her friend Milena, she too was bored with the quiet predictable life on the island. Hence, together they did a lot of exploring around the island as well as the sea.

Milena was proficient in sailing and knew when to tack and when to jibe. She was lucky enough to be able to take her family's sail boat out to sea at any time as long as she first asked for permission. Her parents, Mira and Angelo, didn't worry about Milena taking the boat out to sail. They knew she was a responsible sailor, and normally there wasn't much to worry about as the Adriatic Sea was typically calm because it was sheltered by the Dinaric mountains to the east and by the islands and the Italian alps to the west. The only trickly part was the Pasman Channel (pronounced pash-mon) because of its strong currents that changed every six hours. But those currents were also the reason why that part of the Adriatic Sea was the cleanest with crystal clear water. Her parents told her not to sail through there because the currents could wreak havoc to a boat, even with an experienced captain. One wrong move or moment of distraction was all it took for disaster to happen. But for Milena, going through the channel was the exciting part, so she figured what they didn't know wouldn't hurt them.

"You know what I read?" asked Rosana as they continued walking up the mountain during a lull in the wind. "I read that the Vikings were pirates in medieval Europe. I didn't know that, did you?"

"I knew they were seaborne warriors from Scandinavia, but I didn't know they were pirates that raided and looted," replied Milena.

"Yep, they did that during the Viking age between the 8th and 12th centuries. They raided the coasts, rivers and cities all over Western Europe and in 1202, they invaded Zadar," continued

Rosana. "Can you imagine living in those days? And I also read that after the Romans invaded Dalmatia back in the 9th and 10th centuries, some pirates, called the Narentines, rampantly raided the Adriatic Sea and Dalmatian islands, as well.

"I knew that," said Milena. "My father told me that the Romans had a fort on one of the Kornati Islands that they used not only to store food and wine supplies, but also as a refitment facility for their naval vessels. You know there are 125 Kornati islands. So, there was enough forest on the islands to replace any lumber they needed for their ships. He also said there is a lookout tower on the top of a mountain on our island that served as a lookout for enemies coming to attack the islands. The lookout guard would signal the refitment facility that pirates, or other invaders, were coming. By day, they signaled with smoke and by night they signaled with fire."

"That's interesting," said Rosana. "Sure was exciting living back in those days. Now, nothing happens on the island.

"I'm freezing," said Rosana. "This really was a bad idea, and my eyes are so watery, I can hardly see where I'm going."

"Oh, stop complaining," said Milena. "We are almost there. "Look! I see the entrance to the cave from here."

"I don't see anything except the forest, said Rosana. "How can you see that far?"

"You need glasses," laughed Milena. "It's a huge cave and you still can't make out the entrance?"

Rosana just ignored her to save an argument.

The entrance to the cave was tall enough for them to walk into while standing up rather than to crawl into as in some other caves. Even so, the forest was filled with trees, bramble, and large boulders that camouflaged the cave entrance enough that unless you knew it was there, you'd might miss it.

Milena and Rosana stood at the cave's entrance and shook off the cold. With the natural vegetation, they were slightly shielded from the wind. They rubbed their hands together to warm up while shaking off the chills.

"Brrrr, I'm so cold," said Rosana. Rosana knew that though Milena wouldn't admit it, she too was chilled to the bone.

They took the small flashlights out of their jacket pockets and turned them on. They took a few steps into the cave and both stopped suddenly.

"What is that weird smell?" asked Rosana with her nose scrunched up.

"I don't know," replied Milena whose nose was just as scrunched. "It kinda reminds me of rotting plants. Maybe the winds blew in lots of plant debris that's now rotting inside."

"Ewww. It's almost like animal poop. Oh no. I hope we don't run into a wild boar in there," said Rosana holding her nose.

"Well, I don't hear anything. I'm sure it's fine," said Milena. "Let's keep going."

They walked further into the huge cave. With each step, it got darker despite their little flashlights. Rock formations that looked like icicles hung above them and also grew upward from the ground. The light from their flashlights reflected off the many cobwebs high up on the ceiling, giving the illusion of lace on the cave walls.

Rosana shone her flashlight to the ground to watch her footing. "Hey. Look at these footprints."

Milena walked closer to her. "Yes, it looks like someone was here recently," she said, swinging her flashlight around the cave's main chamber to see if anything else looked out of place, but she didn't notice anything amiss.

They walked carefully so as not to disturb anything.

"I do love the rock icicles,' said Milena with a giggle.

"You do know those rock formations are not icicles, right? They're called stalactites," said Rosana. "And the ones that form on the floor of the cave are called stalagmites."

"Yes, I knew that," replied Milena, rolling her eyes and laughing. "I was just being silly."

"This cave is called Friar's Cave because over the centuries, water dripping from the stalactites onto a rock formed a tall statue that looks like a friar," said Rosana as she shone her flashlight up and down the statue.

"It's awesome, and so tall," said Milena. "It's taller than Steve, so it's well over six feet tall."

They wondered if the pirates ever made it this far up the mountain. They fantasized about any loot that they would have hidden in the cave.

"Can you imagine if we found jeweled necklaces from the 12th century in his cave?" asked Milena.

"What would you do with them, wear them or hide them in a secret hiding place?" answered Rosana with a question.

"I don't really know, maybe I'd try to sell the jewelry," replied Milena. "Or, I would take the jewels out of their settings and just sell the stones, that way, it avoids the antiquities question."

"Not really," said Rosanna. "They cut stones differently in those days so they would still be recognized as ancient stones."

The girls laughed at their own silliness, and continued on their walk. But, as they took a few steps further into the cave, their noses began to scrunch up again. The smell they noticed at the entrance was getting worse. The further they walked into the chamber, the stronger the smell became, to the point the girls had to hold their noses and their stomachs were feeling queasy.

"Oh my God. The smell is so bad here," said Milena. "That's certainly not dead plants."

"I know. It's gross. Maybe an animal died in here," replied Rosana through the handkerchief she had over her nose and mouth.

"I don't think I can stay in here much longer," said Milena.

"I agree. Let's just check out the statute a little more," said Rosana. "As many times as we've seen it, it still amazes me how creative Mother Nature can be."

"Yes, that's incredible," agreed Milena looking up at the statue. By now her eyes were watering from the smell.

Though they've seen the formation before, it still caught their imagination. Rosana was so fascinated by the formation that she ignored the smell. She walked to the backside of the statue to explore it in further detail. But then the effects of the awful smell overwhelmed her, and without warning, she felt her stomach contract as she started to dry heave. Feeling that she was going to throw up, she turned quickly to avoid spewing onto the statue. With a handkerchief in one hand over her mouth and the other on her flashlight, she angled her body to the cave wall. Just then, in the glow of her flashlight, she saw the source of the smell.

On the floor just a mere step away from her, was what looked like a human body. Rosana gasped. In her confusion and shock, she dropped her flashlight and handkerchief. She felt an electric surge pulse through her body as adrenaline pumped through her veins. She had never seen a dead body before and didn't know whether to scream or cry or run. She froze for a moment like a deer in headlights. The fear built inside of her. She stood there in shock for what seemed like hours, but was really only seconds, and then she did the only thing she could think of. She turned to run. To run far away from the smell and the sight of a dead human being. In her frantic attempt to get as far away from the body as possible, she tripped over his outstretched leg and lost her balance. With her arms flailing in the air, she couldn't act fast enough to regain her balance, and she fell face down on top of the body and landed with a hard thud. It felt cold and hard and wet and oozy. The flashlight's beam coming from the floor gave her just enough light to see that the wetness and goo was actually bugs eating the flesh. Unable to contain herself anymore, Rosana let out a blood curdling scream.

The hairs on Milena's neck stood up on end. She had never heard someone scream like that. "Rosana! What happened?" she yelled as she ran toward her friend, aiming her flashlight in the direction of the scream.

"What's wr-" She froze. It took a few seconds for her to process what she saw. But then she realized that Rosana was lying face down on top of a body … a dead body. Flies and other insects were crawling on her friend. A puddle of coagulated blood was on the ground. When the sight in front of her became clear, Milena let out a scream too. She stood there stammering for a moment and then realized she needed to help her friend. She ran to Rosana, grabbed her arm, and helped her up. Rosana immediately started swatting bugs off of herself. They were both shaking and crying.

"Oh my God, oh my God, oh my God," Milena frantically repeated. She examined her friend and said, "You're covered in blood! Did you get hurt?"

"Umm, no, I don't think so," said Rosana, unable to even comprehend the question well. She felt like her skin was crawling and kept swatting off the now imaginary bugs.

"Well at least we know what the smell is now," said Milena, trying to bring some levity to the situation.

"What do we do now?" asked Rosana.

The girls stood quietly for a moment, both nervously looking around the cave, now worried that someone else might be in the cave with them, or even more dead bodies.

"Well, we're here," said Milena. "So I think we should take a closer look."

Rosana nodded. "But don't touch anything," she said. "We're not supposed to touch anything in a crime scene, if that's what this is."

"I think you've already done that," said Milena with a slight chuckle.

Rosana let out a half-hearted laugh, and tried to put on a brave face, though she was still in shock.

The girls walked closer to the body. The adrenaline coursed through their bodies, making the smell somewhat unnoticeable now.

Milena focused her flashlight on the man's body. He was lying face down on the ground. His legs were spread eagle, and his pants pockets were turned inside out as if someone had searched him for something. They had no idea what happened or how long he had been there.

"Look! He was choked to death," said Milena. "There's some kind of wire around his neck. And there's blood under his head and neck area. Whoever chocked him must have cut his jugular vein with the wire."

Rosana picked up her flashlight from the ground and used the dirt from the cave floor to clean off the blood from the flashlight and her hands. She shone it all around them.

"The blood actually squirted over there," said Rosana as she pointed to the streaks of blood on the cave floor. "That's at least two feet away from his body. He must have struggled with someone. I think someone murdered him."

"I think you're right," Milena agreed.

Milena saw her friend's handkerchief on the ground and picked it up. "Your handkerchief is a bit bloody," said Milena as she held it up for Rosana to see.

"Leave it, I don't want it," said Rosana. "I never want to be reminded of this sight ever again."

They both backed away from the body.

"We have to report this to the police," said Milena. "Don't touch anything and let's get the heck outta here! This body gives me the creeps."

"You don't have to tell me twice," said Rosana as they ran quickly out of the cave.

They nervously made their way down the mountain being careful to mind where they were going. Between the wind and their desire to get as far away as possible from the body, it was easy to lose one's concentration and balance.

After several minutes, Rosana broke the silence. "I've been thinking about that wire," she said. "Whoever did this must have been wearing leather gloves; otherwise, they wouldn't have been able to twist that wire behind his neck like that. They would have cut their fingers."

"You actually noticed the twisted wire?" asked Milena.

"I was laying right on top of the man," retorted Rosana. "I was looking right at it, though I wish I'd never seen it. Now I'm going to have nightmares about this."

It was actually more of a danger walking down the mountain than it was walking up. Now, the wind was working against them by blowing right into their faces, which slowed them down; and when a strong gust came their way, they had to stop walking and brace themselves by getting low to the ground in order to not be pushed backward and possibly fall flat on their backs. Their hoods were useless against the wind as it whipped the hoods and their hair around wildly which made it even more difficult to see where they were going. It was blowing so hard that it was difficult to even hold a conversation without yelling.

As soon as they saw Steve's house in the distance, they started gingerly trotting toward it. They knew Steve would know what to do.

The dogs started barking well before they approached Steve's door. "Steve! Open up!" yelled Milena as she lifted her fist to bang on the door. But just then, Steve flung the door open.

Steve stood there with a confused look on his face. "What happened? Are you alright?" he asked. "You look like you've seen a ghost. And Rosana, what happened to you?" he asked as he led them inside the house and sat them at the table in the kitchen.

Rosana started talking frantically, "We were up in the cave and I fell on top of a dead body and it smelled really bad and there were bugs and the guy had a wire around his neck and there was blood and I fell on him and it was so gross…." She started crying and was talking so fast that Steve could hardly keep up.

"Wait. What? …. Slow down now. What's this about a dead body? Why is there blood all over you?"

Milena hugged her friend and tried to calm her down. Once Milena felt Rosana relax, she let go, took a deep breath, and told Steve everything in the calmest way she could.

Steve's eyes popped open at what he was hearing. "Okay. Let me get this straight. There's a dead human body in the cave? And you think he was murdered? Is that right?"

"Yes," said Milena. "That's right."

Look at me!" cried Rosana capriciously through teary eyes. "How else would I have all this blood on me? I've got the creeps just thinking about how he was strangled with that wire. Who would do such an evil thing, and why?"

Steve was too bewildered at what he heard and tried very hard to make sense of it. He tried to comfort them by having them do some deep breathing exercises to calm them down. He also gave them some chamomile tea to help calm their nerves.

"You need to tell the police everything," he said. "Do you want me to go with you?"

They both shook their heads.

"No," Rosana said. "We can do it ourselves. We'll call them as soon as we get to the pay phone in the village."

"Are you sure?" asked Steve. "This is a big deal."

"We know," replied Milena. "We've got this."

"You girls are very brave," he said. Then he hugged them goodbye and watched them as they walked down the mountain.

There were no police stations on the island. The closest one was in Preko on the island of Ugljan (meaning olive island and pronounced oo-glon), the next island to the north, Preko literally means 'over' as in 'cross over.' The village was aptly named as it is in Preko that people took the car ferry to get to the mainland city of Zadar. The two closest mainland cities were Zadar to the north of Ugljan island and Biograd to the south of Pasman island. There was also a ferry at the south end of Pasman in the village of Tkon (pronounced coon), which took passengers to Biograd.

The old walled city of Zadar with its beautiful Roman architecture was now filled with shops, restaurants, and cafes and was mostly a tourist attraction, with its 9th century St. Donatus church and the famous sea organ, which produced beautiful ocean music with each lap of the gentle waves. The 'Salutation to the Sun' solar light show, adjacent to the steps of the sea organ, produced rhythmic multi colored lights on the glass floor by the edge of the sea. During the day the solar cells captured the sun's energy which is released at night as a light show. People walked and danced on that glass floor, some in rhythm to the flashing lights. Both were produced by the gentle lapping waves. This was the only one of its kind in the world. Though Biograd was also filled with shops, restaurants and cafes, it was where the courts were located and where people went to deal with legal matters such as land ownership.

When they got to their village, they rushed straight for the public pay phone, which was located by the post office in the center of the village. As they ran frantically down the main street, some of the older people yelled at them to slow down. Once at the phone, they debated who should make the call.

"You probably should do it since you're the one who fell on the body," said Milena.

"No. You should do it," Rosana said. "You were much calmer telling Steve about it. I'll probably ramble on again."

They agreed that Milena would make the call. Since they didn't have any money with them for the phone, they used the local emergency number. Milena's hands shook as she punched in 1-1-2 to call for help.

Ring … Ring … Ring…

"Preko police station, Officer Hrenek speaking," a deep voice greeted.

"Hello," Milena began. "I need help. My friend and I were up in the cave on the mountain by Nevidane. We found something …" She paused and looked around. She saw villagers walking past going about their business. She didn't want them to hear what she was telling the police, so she lowered her voice and practically whispered into the phone, "We found a dead body. We think there's been a murder in the cave."

"A murder? In Nevidane? Well, are you sure? That type of thing never happens here," the officer said with a slight chuckle.

"Yes, I'm sure," said Milena. "This isn't a prank call and I wish you'd treat it seriously."

"What are your names? You sound very young. How old are you?"

"I'm sixteen, but what does that have anything to do with it?" asked Milena.

The officer ignored her question and asked, "And who are your parents?"

Milena gave the police officer everything he asked for.

"Did you touch or move anything?" he asked.

"No … well ... not on purpose. My friend fell and landed on the body. That's how we found it."

"Mmm-huh," was all the police officer said.

"How do you know he was dead?" asked the officer.

"There was a wire around his neck and blood everywhere and insects and flies on his body and the smell was awful!" said Milena rushing her words.

She heard his pen scribbling notes.

"Okay," he continued. "We'll come tomorrow morning. It's too windy now, he's not going anywhere since he's dead, and it will be dark soon. We can't get up the mountain in the dark. I'll meet you tomorrow at the village square at around 8 o'clock. If this is a joke and you're not there, I'll go to your parents' home and give them a visit. Understand?"

"Yes, sir, this isn't a joke. I'm as serious as a heart attack," Milena added, worried that the officer might not take the call seriously. Then she hung up.

Since the island was small, the police knew where almost everyone lived. There were very few paved roads and there were no street names or house numbers. It was like stepping back in time 200 years. In fact, in their village, everyone knew where everyone else lived. The main road running the length of the island was paved. And in their village, the main street was paved and there was one paved road at each of the two entrances to the village that connected to the main road. Almost all other roads were dirt roads.

As they walked home, the two friends speculated what could have possibly happened to cause someone to murder a person.

"This is such a small island," said Rosana. "Only about two thousand people live here full time on the whole island, so it isn't hard to know your neighbors. We know everyone in our village. Do you think he was someone who lived here? Or a visitor?"

"I don't know.," said Milena. "I was so scared when we discovered him that I wasn't about to stick around to turn the corpus over to see if I recognized him. Plus, from watching TV, I know better than to disturb the scene of a crime."

They both had wild speculations about the events that led up to the murder, but that's all they were—just wild speculations with no facts to back them up.

Milena and Rosana parted ways after a short walk and went to their respective homes to have dinner with their families. Milena conveyed the story of what happened in the cave to her parents. Her mother, Mira, was outraged at the thought that someone would actually murder another person and in such a cruel and evil way.

"I can't believe what I'm hearing," she blurted out in disbelief. "This is such a safe island. Nothing like this ever happens here. I'm just sorry you had to be the ones to discover it. Are you alright, dear?" she asked her daughter as she took Milena's head into both of her hands and lowered it to her shoulder to give her a big comforting motherly hug.

"Yes, Mom, I'm okay. It's Rosana who tripped over the man's leg and fell on top of him," said Milena. "She was so scared Mom. She said she was going to have nightmares over this. She's the one I feel sorry for."

"Don't worry sweetheart," said Angelo, her father. "The police will do an investigation and have a reasonable explanation of what happened. Rosana is a strong girl. She'll feel better after the police do their investigation. I'm just relieved that you're both safe and nothing happened to you on that mountain."

Angelo was a medium height, muscular man in his mid-fifties with graying hair and brown eyes. Unlike some of the men on the island who chose to become merchant marines, he chose to remain on the island and to farm the family land. He worked hard in the fields for very little monetary reward, but he was happy in life. He was able to put healthy food on the table for his family, he had a loving wife, and trusted his daughter implicitly.

Mira, his wife, was in her early fifties, a bit on the heavy side and was slightly shorter than Angelo, and had light brown hair and brown eyes. Her salt and pepper hair was pulled up in a bun at the back of her head. She wore an apron that looped around her neck and tied in the back. Mira was an excellent cook and baker, and she sold some of her pastries at the local farmer's market. They both worked their land and still lived off the land and the sea just as their ancestors did for centuries before them.

Angelo and Mira's house was typical of the other older houses on the island. Their house was made of stone and the entry to the house had a high solid wooden gate which they keep closed for privacy. Opening the gate revealed a peaceful concrete courtyard with brightly colored flowers along the parameter and in pots. In the center of the courtyard was a table where they ate their evening meals in the summer time. Directly across from the entry was an outdoor kitchen called the black kitchen. It was attached to the main house and that's where most meals were cooked in the summer so as not to overheat the main house. It was called the black kitchen because over time the walls turned black from cooking on the open flame with coal and wood. This one-pot method of roasting food was called 'under the bell' cooking and was a very popular way to roast meat, or fish, with potatoes and green vegetables. To the left of the outdoor kitchen were stairs going to the second level. The large front room served as a parlor to greet guests. Right next to the parlor was the large, eat-in indoor kitchen, which was the heart of the home where everything took place. There was no dining room, so everyone ate either in the kitchen or overflowed into the parlor. The other two rooms on the ground floor were a bathroom and a smaller sized room for watching television. The upstairs had three bedrooms. Most of the interior floors were white marble including the stairs, and throw rugs covered the tile floors in the bedrooms. As was the tradition, their home was large enough to accommodate a second family because it was customary for a groom and his bride to live in the groom's parents' house until they could afford to build a house of their own.

When Rosana got home, both her mother and father were upset because they saw that she was covered with blood. Her father had a scornful look on his face, and her mother's eyes were opened almost as wide as her mouth in disbelief of Rosana's appearance.

Her father Marko, a merchant marine, was a shorter, huskier man of about 5 foot 8 inches and he had dark brown hair, which had begun to recede, and brown eyes. He also had a tattoo of an anchor on his right upper arm. He was a merchant marine, and as such, he was rarely home. He decided to go into that line of work because it was one way to earn a good living to support a family, see the world, and to have a good pension once he retired. This happened to be one of those times when he wasn't at sea.

His captain was a very strict man who demanded loyalty from his crew. That's one of the reasons why Rosana's father was so tough on her. She understood that and knew he would be back at sea soon, so she tried not to pay him much mind, but sometimes that was easier said than done. It was a vicious circle. The more he was away, the more distant she became from him, and the more distant she became, the more he wanted to be loved and respected by her. He didn't know any other way to deal with her except to demand respect and rule with an iron hand, which wasn't working very well.

But there was another profound reason her father was so strict with Rosana. While Rosana was an only child, it wasn't always that way. At one time she had a little sister, Danica, but she died a few years earlier. Danica's death was devastating to Rosana's parents, especially to her father. Maybe it was because he felt guilty that he wasn't there when it happened. He was in Rio de Janeiro Brazil at the time, and couldn't even get back in time for the funeral. Danica died when the girls were with their mom digging for clams near the Pasman Channel. She was four years younger than Rosana, and didn't know how to swim. The strong current of the Pasman Channel sucked her down and then swept her away before Ana could get to her. The guilt Marko felt enveloped him, but he didn't want anyone to know. In fact, being strict, stern, and demanding was his way of masking the pain he felt every day.

Rosana's mother, Ana, was slightly shorter than her father. Ana had brown hair and hazel eyes. She was a slim woman who had a very erect posture considering she worked in the fields most days. She and Rosana were cut from the same cloth as they both longed for adventure. Many times, Ana would go sailing with her husband when he was home, just for the thrill of the open sea. She dreamt of faraway places that she knew she'd never get to experience. But, her life on the island was a good and satisfying life. She didn't wish to live anywhere else as she was happy there. However, secretly, she wished she could visit places like France and Spain, but for now, she'd have to be satisfied just reading about them.

"What on earth happened to you, Rosana?" yelled her father. "You're covered in blood! What trouble did you get into this time, huh?"

"Oh dear God," said her mother, in almost a whisper. "What happened honey? Are you alright? Whose blood is that?"

Rosana explained what happened at the cave as calmly as she could while still holding back tears. Her father was furious, as she knew he would be.

"I can't believe you went up the mountain today in the bura. You're a stupid girl and you're always doing stupid things like going up to that cave. I knew you were up to no good when you didn't come home all day. We were wondering where you were. You could have been killed in that bura for all we knew, you idiot!" he hollered.

"Now, Marko, she had nothing to do with the dead body. She wasn't up to no good. She just happened to stumble across the body. It's not her fault, for Christ sakes. Stop yelling at her!" retorted her mother in defense of Rosana.

After being yelled at by her father, Rosana couldn't control her tears any longer. The stress of the entire cave incident and the tongue lashing she got from father was just too much for her to take. She ran off to her room to change her clothes, with her mother close behind.

"Honey, don't let your father upset you. You've done nothing wrong and you know he loves you and means well. Come here," she said pulling Rosana close to her chest and kissing her forehead while hugging her. "You just take a hot shower and get into your PJs. I'll bring you a plate of food and you can eat it in here. I know you're exhausted and need to sleep. You know how your father is. He'll come to his senses and then try to make it up to you in his awkward way," said Ana smiling at her daughter trying to put her mind at ease.

Rosana yearned for a loving and trusting relationship with her father like the one Milena and her father had, but that was not to be.

A GRUESOME SIGHT

By the next morning, the winds had died down considerably. At 8am sharp, the girls met each other in the village square to see if the officers had arrived yet, but no one was there.

"Good morning, Milena," said Rosana, feeling much better than she did yesterday. "What did your parents say about what happened in the cave?" she inquired.

"They were worried about me, and they were very stunned to learn there was a murder on the island," answered Milena. "They couldn't believe the ordeal we, and especially you, went through. How about your parents? What did they say?"

"I'd rather not talk about it," said Rosana.

"Was it that bad, Rosana?" asked Milena with concern. "Did he hit you? Come on, please tell me."

"Well, my mom was supportive and tried to comfort me, but my dad was a total jerk," replied Rosana with her head and eyes looking down at the ground. Her hands were in her pants pockets as she slid her right foot from right to left and back again as if to brush away the pain.

"Why? What did he say now?" prodded Milena.

"Oh, he called me stupid again, like he always does, and yelled at me for being on the mountain in the bura," replied Rosana still sliding her right foot back and forth.

"Don't take it to heart Rosana. Think about where he is coming from. He is worried about your wellbeing. He lost one daughter already and he is scared of losing you too," said Milena. "You're the only child now and so he is just being over protective. You know he loves you."

"I guess you're right," replied Rosana. "I didn't think of it that way."

In an effort to change the subject, Rosana said, "I wonder what's keeping the police. They should have been here by now. I hope they didn't blow us off as a prank call."

There were only two ways into the village from the main road, at either the north end or south end of the village, and both roads led to the village center. At one entrance, there was a huge cross supposedly to ward off evil spirits. In the center of the village was a monument left behind from communism days where now traditional Christmas holiday celebrations took place.

As she looked at the monument, Milena thought back to past Christmases and how the men of the village lit a bon fire every year in keeping with an old tradition. They'd go up to the mountain and cut down an evergreen pine tree. They'd bring it back to the village center, and on Christmas Eve, they'd walk in circles around the tree as they sang the centuries old song depicting the many deaths that happened in the village during an ancient time back before the Middle Ages. On Christmas Eve, they'd light the tree on fire and take turns stoking the fire all night and day up until Three Kings Day (January 6th), also known as little Christmas. The fire burned eternal during that time.

The villagers kept the tradition alive in order to honor the many people who died during that time. Many believed evil spirts were to blame for the deaths, hence the cross at the entrance of the village. As one village farmer liked to point out, "It was just two legged creatures that died and not the animals." According to the story, the villagers were so scared of the evil spirits that one man went to his rooftop and chanted over and over to the heavens, "Kill the four-legged, not the two-legged." Then, according to local lore, all the four-legged animals died, but the people and the chickens survived. This superstitious tradition never died, and each year the villagers sang a song about the Neviska Koleda (Nevidane's Christmas) while circling the fire. They decorated the village center with Christmas lights and the women of the town brought pastries and wine to the village center where the residents would come by to extend their holiday wishes and partake in the food and drinks. Even though the tradition sounded a little morbid, Milena thought it was the loveliest time of year. She especially liked how everyone got together to sing Christmas carols at night in front of the bonfire. That's where the girls decided to wait, as they had a good view of anyone coming into the village from the main road.

"Milena," said Rosana in a stern voice. "Are you daydreaming again? "Ha-ha-ha. Where were you just now?"

"Oh, sorry," said Milena. "Yes, I was daydreaming."

"Not about pirates, again, I hope," said Rosana.

"No, just about our Christmas tradition," replied Milena. "Do you think it's based on truth? Why do you suppose all the four-legged animals died?"

"I don't know," replied Rosana. "Maybe it was some kind of animal flu. We'll never know."

"I know. It's weird to me how our older folks are still so superstitious in this day and age," said Milena.

The village center consisted of an old church that wasn't actually used anymore since a new larger and more modern church had been built just down the road. There was also a post office, a small grocery store, and a fish stand where the fisherman would sell their daily catch. But you had to get there early in the morning; otherwise, the fish would all be gone. Croatians ate a lot of fish!

Two of the favorite ways to prepare fish were to grill it on an open fire or to make a one pot brudet (fish stew). Brudet was traditionally made with a variety of different white fish and some versions of the brudet also included shell fish such as clams, mussels, scallops, shrimps and even squid, much like the Italian Zuppa di Pesce dish.

At about 8:15 they saw the police car approaching. As they watched the car get closer and closer, they both felt a knot in their stomachs.

"I'm nervous," Rosana whispered to her friend.

"Don't be," said Milena. "We didn't do anything."

Two police officers got out of the car and made their way toward the girls. The older one, Officer Hrenek, looked to be in his fifties. He was a tall stocky man of about six feet with brown hair and brown eyes and his beer belly hung over his pants belt. He sported a chevron mustache and wore glasses. The younger one, Officer Radic, was a clean-shaven man, slightly shorter than Officer Hrenek, and probably in his thirties. He had black hair and dark blue eyes and was brutely handsome. As soon as Milena saw him, she immediately wondered if he'd ever thought of becoming a model instead of going into law enforcement. She also wondered if he was single as she didn't see a wedding band on his finger.

Both officers wore the official police uniform of navy-blue pants and a light blue short slevved shirt with their name patch on one of the two shirt pockets. On the right sleeve there was a patch depicting the Croatian flag. Underneath that patch was another one in the shape of a badge with the word 'Policija' and an official police emblem right beneath it on the same patch.

"Good morning, are you girls Milena and Rosana?" asked Officer Hrenek.

"Good morning, officers, Yes, I'm Milena and this is my friend Rosana," replied Milena.

So, you're the girls that reported the murder?"

"Yes, up in the cave," replied Milena.

"Where are your parents?"

"We didn't know that you wanted them to come to the cave with us," replied Milena. "We thought that since they weren't at the scene of the crime, there was no reason to have them come along."

"Well, you thought wrong," said Officer Hrenek rudely. "We want to talk to them as well. But, never mind now. We will talk to them when we return from the cave. Let's get started. Lead the way."

The girls led the officers up the mountain trail that they took the day before rather than to have the officers drive up the north road, as the north road didn't go far enough to reach the cave and the cave was on the other side of the mountain.

The walk up the mountain was a bit strenuous on Officer Hrenek, who looked flushed in the face and breathed heavily as he was out of breath rather quickly. He wasn't in great shape and since he didn't often leave his car to chases anyone or to walk up a mountain, he had to stop a few times along the way. Officer Radic and the girls accommodated his frequent stops. Officer Radic didn't say much. He looked around at the tranquil and beautiful view of the sea below him as he didn't often get an opportunity to be on that mountain.

Officer Hrenek was clearly annoyed that he had to make this arduous walk up the mountain. His furrowed brow looked to be a permanent expression on his face, and his frequent and heavy sighs and huffs made his disgust apparent.

"And you girls did this during the bura? How on earth did you not fall?" The question was rhetorical. As Milena started to answer, he motioned with his hand as if to say, "Never mind. I don't want to know." By the time they were within sight of the compound, Officer Hrenek was soaked from sweat.

As they approached Steve's compound, the barking dogs greeted them, as did Steve.

The younger officer, Radic, didn't say much. He left all the questioning to Officer Hrenek.

Officer Hrenek skipped the pleasantries and went right into questioning Steve.

"You must be Steve, the hermit, am I right?" asked Hrenek, "I've heard a lot about you through the grapevine,"

"Yes, I'm Steve, but I don't think I'd classify myself as a hermit. I do get into town occasionally, and I know some of the locals. I just happen to like living up here with this beautiful view. Anything wrong with that?" asked Steve smiling.

"I didn't mean to offend you, Steve. Sorry if I did," said Hrenek. "But we do have a few questions for you. Did you see anything out of the ordinary up here in the last few days?"

"Only these two coming up here in the bura," said Steve with a slight chuckle.

"Yes, we found that a bit unusual as well. But this is no joking matter. According to these girls, a serious crime was committed up there."

"I was teasing for Christ's sake," said Steve. "The girls come up here all the time."

"And you didn't hear or see anything?" asked Hrenek.

"No," replied Steve.

"What about your dogs? Did they bark at anything unusual?" Hrenek continued with the questioning.

"Not really. If you know dogs, you know they have different barks for different circumstances. They're dogs. They bark at a lot of things, but I didn't hear them barking in a way that would have alerted me to a situation that needed my attention."

The officers looked at him with a sneer. "We'll be back with more questions if we have any," said Officer Hrenek. He then turned to the girls and said, "Take us to the cave now."

As they walked further up the mountain, Hrenek sighed a loud audible sigh that made Milena and Rosana smile at each other.

"Hrenek sure is having a hard time keeping up with us, isn't he?" whispered Milena to Rosana as she glanced behind her to see how far back the officer was. Rosana nodded in agreement. She was afraid to say anything negative as she didn't want Hrenek to overhear her. Radic stayed at Hrenek's side and walked at the same pace as Hrenek. It looked like they were conversing, but the girls couldn't hear what they were saying. The more the officers talked, the more anxious the girls got.

"Why are we worrying about this? We didn't do anything wrong," said Milena.

"I don't know. That officer sure is gruff with us. It's as if he's convinced we had something to do with it," said Rosana in a worrisome voice.

When the girls reached the entrance of the cave, they waited for the officers to catch up. By then, Officer Hrenek was panting. His chest was heaving so hard that he couldn't speak very well. The girls tired hard to keep from cracking a smile.

Upon walking into the cave, the stench hit them like a wave. "Ohhhh, geez," said Hrenek. "You smelled that and still went in anyway?" he asked as the sweat poured off him. Milena couldn't tell if he was sweating because of the walk or because of the over-powering stench. She suspected it was a little of both.

"Well, it wasn't that bad yesterday," said Milena gagging on her words. Her face was all scrunched up and her mouth started to water as the contents of her stomach churned and made its way to her throat.

The officers turned on their high-powered flashlights and made their way into the cave. As they approached the body, Radic gasped at the sight. That was something he didn't mean to do in front of the girls, but the condition of the dead man's body caught him totally off guard. He hadn't ever seen a body in as bad a shape as this one. The bugs and rats in the cave ate through much of the dead man's flesh and the sight of it made him gag.

Rosana was nowhere to be seen. She took one look at the corpse and ran outside to throw up. She was totally disgusted by what she saw. Chills ran up her spine and literally made her shake. And as much as she tried, she couldn't overcome the gag instinct. Radic followed right behind her. He had to get some fresh air. Both of them threw up in disgust. Milena and Hrenek followed shortly after as they too were sick to their stomachs. Milena tried very hard not to think about what she saw because every time she did, she had the dry heaves.

Officer Radic tied a handkerchief around his nose and mouth and went back inside to take pictures of the dead body and the surrounding area. Hrenek stayed outside with the girls and began questioning them about the details of how they came upon the body.

"Why were you on the mountain during a bura?" he asked gruffly. "What was so urgent that you had to risk your life to get up to the cave?"

"There was no urgency," said Milena, clearly irritated by the tone of the officer's voice. "As Steve told you, we come up to the mountain often. Ask anyone and they will tell you that we love coming up here. We were just bored, that's all."

"But during a bura? Did your mother drop you on your head when you were a baby?" he sarcastically asked.

"No!" said Milena annoyed. "We are very familiar with the mountain and we like adventure. Clearly the bura didn't bother us much since we're standing here unscathed, which is more than I can say about you." She couldn't help herself. She always made snide comments like that and then would say, "It's not me that gets me into trouble; it's my mouth."

Looking Milena over intently, the officer then said in a demanding voice, "Let me see your hands and your forearms."

Milena couldn't believe he asked her that, but she obliged and stuck out her arms and opened her hands. He carefully examined Milena's hands, her finger nails, and forearms for scratches in great detail, but said nothing.

With that the officer turned to Rosana, who had been quiet until now, and said sternly, "And I want to see your hands and arms as well."

Rosana was scared, but she wasn't about to let this officer try to pin anything on her. So, she showed him her hands and her forearms. Since the officer didn't say anything to her either, Rosana blurted out, "God, you don't think we did it, do you?" As soon as the words left her lips, she wanted to pull them back.

The officer was in the middle of writing something down on his pad and, without lifting his head up, he looked up at her over the top of his horn-rimmed glasses and gave her a disgusted look, but he didn't say a word.

With that, Officer Radic came out of the cave looking green again. In his hand was a clear baggie containing a handkerchief. He spoke for the first time since they came to the cave.

"Do you know whose handkerchief this is?" he asked while looking at the girls.

"That's mine," said Rosana. "I dropped it, along with my flashlight, yesterday when I fell on the body."

"And why were you up here in the first place?" asked Radic.

"Officer Hrenek already asked us that," said Rosana.

"And you told him, but not me. Tell me why you were up in the cave and on such a windy day, no less," insisted Radic.

"As we told your partner, we always come up here. And, no the bura did not stop us. We had no ulterior motive for coming up here. We just liked the challenge. That's all," said Rosana.

"You say you come up here all the time. Were you here last week prior to finding the dead body?" asked Radic.

"No," replied Rosana. "Both Milena and I were in Zagreb visiting Milena's cousin. Ask my parents if you don't believe me." Now Rosana was totally convinced that the officers were trying to pin this murder on her and her friend. *'But, why?'* she thought. *'There is no evidence that we had anything to do with it. Surely a handkerchief isn't proof that we murdered someone. What are these cops up to?'*

After the officers were done investigating the crime scene and finished questioning the girls, they all walked back down the mountain with one officer in the front and the other in the rear. Rosana turned to Milena with a worried look on her face.

"I think they suspect us, and mostly me. Do we need a lawyer?" asked Rosana.

"No, I don't think so, not unless they charge us with something," said Milena. "But I don't know what you're worried about. I keep telling you, WE DIDN'T DO ANYTHING WRONG."

"I'm sorry we even called the police," said Rosana. "We should have just left and let someone else find the body. Now they think we had something to do with this murder and they'll want to question our parents. This is terrible."

As Hrenek stated earlier, he did want to question their parents. The officers escorted Milena and Rosana to Milena's parents' house first. Upon arriving there, Hrenek wasted no time in questioning Angelo. But the officer didn't get the warm reception he was hoping for.

"Angelo, where were you yesterday during the bura?" asked Hrenek.

"I was here at home with my wife, why?" answered Angelo.

"You were both here and you didn't think it was strange that your daughter Milena wasn't at home?" he asked.

Angelo gave the officer an earful. "My daughter and her friend are very responsible young ladies. They go up the mountain just about every chance they get. They bring back herbs, vegetables and fruit that grows wild up there. They never give me a reason to worry. You are barking up the wrong tree, Officer, if you think they had anything to do with this murder. They are only sixteen years old, for crying out loud. If you have evidence to detain them, show it to me, otherwise, please be on your way."

"We will leave … for now," said Officer Hrenek. "But none of you are to leave the island. Do you understand?"

They all nodded.

"We'll be in touch with more questions, I'm sure," said Hrenek.

With that, Officer Radic extended his business card to Angelo and then both officers escorted Rosana home where they intended to question her parents as well.

"The nerve of them even suggesting that you girls had anything to do with the murders," said Mira, Milena's mother, clearly irritated at the officers.

"Don't you worry!" Angelo said. "If they come back to accuse you of anything, I'll get the best lawyer I can find."

Meanwhile, at Rosana's parents' house, Hrenek had the same type of questioning for her parents.

Rosana, knowing how her father tended to overreact, dreaded the police coming to her parents with questions because, somehow, her father would find some fault for which to blame her.

"Marko, where was your daughter last week?" asked Hrenek.

"She was in Zagreb with Milena," answered Marko.

"And why were they in Zagreb?" asked Hrenek.

"They were visiting Milena's cousin," said Marko. "Why are you asking about last week?"

"We just wondered if you knew where your daughter was at all times. We found it strange that your daughter and her friend were up at the cave yesterday," he said. "Did you know your daughter was up there during a bura?"

"No, we didn't," interjected Ana forcefully in defense of Rosana. "But we do know that the girls do a lot of exploring around the island. It's an island, after all. How much trouble can they get into on an island? Why, exactly, are you asking these questions? Surely, you don't suspect them of the murder, do you?"

"We leave no stone unturned, ma'am. We're just doing our job," replied Radic. "And regardless of whether it's an island or not, teenagers tend to get into a lot of trouble. Parents need to do a better job at keeping tabs on their kids."

"I think that was uncalled for, Officer," said Marko, much to Rosana's surprise. "Our Rosana never gets into trouble, and she is not in any way responsible for this crime. How dare you even suggest it."

Rosana tried hard to hold in the chuckle that was threating to leave her lips. She never thought her father would defend her, but she sure was glad he did.

"Here is our card. Call us if you think of anything else, no matter how insignificant you may think it is, Okay?" said Radic.

"Yes, we'll call," replied Marko.

With that, the officers left.

— — —

Later that afternoon, the police officers returned to the village with the coroner. Having the police visit the village twice in one day was unheard of. So naturally some of the villagers were curious as to what was going on. Rumors spread like wildfire in such a small community. Numerous people approached the officers and asked for an explanation.

"Officer, what's going on? Are the girls in trouble? Why is the coroner here? Did someone die?"

"Please everyone, we are not at liberty to discuss any details as of yet. As soon as we know something, we will let you know. Everyone, please, do not follow us up the mountain," Officer Hrenek said to the group. "Please let us do our jobs."

Everyone listened and did as they were told, but that didn't stop the rumor mill from churning.

Several hours later, the officers and coroner returned from the mountain carrying the covered body on a stretcher. Under the white sheet that draped the corpse, people could see the outline of a human body. The officers set the stretcher down on the ground in the village square. A crowd of about 20 people gathered around them. Milena and Rosana were front and center.

"Everyone, may I have your attention please," said Officer Hrenek in his most assertive and loudest voice he could muster. "I'm going to pull down the sheet to see if anyone knows who this man is. I'm going to warn you, though, that his body has not been cleaned up and what you see may be disturbing. So if you have a weak stomach, you may not want to look." With that, he pulled the sheet down to reveal the man's face.

A few of the women gasped. The men leaned in for a closer look. No one came forward with any identifying information about the man.

After people started walking away, Officer Hrenek pulled Milena and Rosana aside.

"I have some good news for you girls," he said smiling. "The coroner estimated the time of death to have been about a week ago. Based on what you told me yesterday, you were both off island in Zagreb during that time. So you have an alibi and are off the hook. We also found a large set of boot prints and partial finger prints. But still, don't leave the island until we have fully completed the investigation and have identified the body," he said shaking his finger at them. "If you have any more information to share with us, please call me."

For the rest of the day the villagers were abuzz with the news of the girls finding a dead body in the cave. The teenagers were practically celebrities. Milena and Rosana didn't quite know what to make of all the attention. No matter where they went, people stopped them and asked questions. *"What was it like to find a dead body?" "Were you scared?" "Did you throw up?"* The girls did their best to politely answer and move along so as not to invite more questions. Of course, they were very glad that the officers had enough evidence to conclude that they hadn't committed the crime.

That night as they sat in Milena's yard drinking sok (a type of flavored sparkling beverage made from fruit) and unwinding from the day, Rosana blurted out, "I think we should go back up the mountain tomorrow to do our own investigation. I don't trust those Mickey Mouse cops."

"I think you're right," Milena said. "I mean, think about it … the dead man was a total stranger, and none of the tourists or ex-pats on the island filed a missing person's report. The last time there was a murder on the island was right after WWII, a long time ago. It's now 2009. That's over 60 years ago! This island is one of the safest places on the planet. Who could have done this?"

"Right? And who was the mysterious dead man?" asked Rosana. "He wasn't native to the island, so why haven't any of the tourists reported a missing person? What was he doing in the cave? Did he know the cave was there, or did he just stumble upon it? … Or did someone lure him there for the sole purpose of killing him?"

These questions and more were percolating in the minds of both girls. So much for it being a boring island.

- 3 -

THE MYSTERY DEEPENS

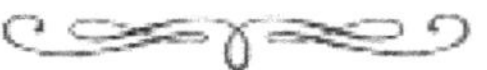

The next day, Milena and Rosana headed back up the mountain to start their own investigation into the mysterious murder. As they walked, their noses caught the scents of the wild herbs and flowers. The fragrances of lavender, sage, fennel, rosemary, thyme, St. John's wort, roses, and pine waffled through the air as the calming aroma washed over them. They also plucked and ate figs from the wild fig trees along the way. Most times when they went to the mountain, they would pick some of the herbs and fruit that grew wild to take home. Fig trees, olive trees, and berry bushes were easy to find. In addition to the better-known types of berries, there were also exotic berries such as chokeberries, goji berry, honeysuckle, currant, and elderberry along the way. But this time, they were on a mission. There was no time to stop to smell the roses.

As usual, as they approached the ancient village on the mountain, Butch, the German Shepard, and the other dogs began to bark before the girls were even in sight. They always carried dog biscuits with them and today was no exception. Butch and his pack took the dog biscuits and continued barking as soon as they gulped them down. Steve came out to see what the commotion was about.

"I thought you two might be coming back," he said. "Did you hear any further news about the corpse?"

The girls told Steve what the officers said about the police finding footprints and partial finger prints.

"Officer Hrenek said that since we were in Zagreb during the time the murder took place, that we are off the hook," said Milena.

"Unbelievable that they would even suspect either of you," said Steve. "Why do you suppose they thought you had anything to do with this murder?"

"I'm not sure," replied Rosana. "But they seemed to hone in on the handkerchief I dropped by the body and the fact that we were up here during a bura. Somehow that convinced them that we were guilty."

"Yes, that's like saying 2 plus 2 equals 22," said Steve. "It's nonsense. But I'm glad that they decided you were off the hook."

"Did you see anyone coming up this way since yesterday?" asked Milena.

"No, no one came this way. You know my dogs would have alerted me if there was anyone even approaching my compound," said Steve as he petted his dogs.

"That's for sure," said Milena. "Those dogs sure have a great sense of smell. You'd think by now they would not bark at us anymore, especially since they know our smell, but they do, every single time without fail."

"The only thing I could think of is that if someone did go up to the cave, they came up from either the north or the west side of the mountain. My dogs wouldn't have heard anyone approaching from those directions," said Steve.

They chatted a bit further, bid their farewells and the girls continued up the mountain. After they walked a bit further, they decided to take a break. They each grabbed a fig from a fig tree before sitting down underneath it in the shady grass. As they ate the figs, they looked out over the tranquil deep blue velvet sea and, thanks to the bura, a cloudless sky. The air was crisp and clean—the kind of day that makes a person glad to be alive.

"You can really smell the fragrant herbs and flowers on a day like today," said Milena. "That's another reason I love coming up here. It's as if the whole world is at peace."

"Look at all the sail boats. I think everyone is out on the sea enjoying this cool weather," said Rosana.

"It's beautiful from up here, like a picture postcard," said Milena. "But, come on, we need to get going."

When the girls got to the cave, they studied it with a new pair of eyes since they were now looking for clues that might lead them to the identity of the dead man they discovered.

Before entering, they carefully checked the area surrounding the cave. They looked for footprints, broken twigs and branches, and they studied the ground for flattened out grass, weeds or other growth, or rocks that may have been disturbed or moved. Then they proceeded to go into the cave.

"Look for any signs that someone else was here, signs of a scuffle, a piece of cloth, blood… anything out of the ordinary," said Rosana as she pulled her flashlight out of her jacket pocket.

"Honestly, I don't know what you expect to find," said Milena. "If the police didn't find anything, what makes you think we will?"

"I told you. I think those cops are a bunch of idiots," replied Rosana. "The officers tried to accuse us of strangling that man. How ridiculous. They think just because we found the body that we committed the crime, and I wouldn't put it past them to try to arrest us if they can't find the person who actually killed that poor guy."

"But they have no evidence that we did anything," said Milena.

"They've been known to frame innocent people and make their lives miserable," replied Rosana impatiently, just on circumstantial evidence. You know how this island is. Nothing much happens here. The worst that happens is people get drunk and start fighting, or there is a fender bender on the main road. That's the extent of it. And, frankly, there was never any need for a police station to be on the island…until now. I refuse to let them pin this on us. We need to solve this crime to prove our innocence. So, come on, keep looking. Look in every nook and corner. Look behind rocks and on boulder ledges."

With that, they went about examining the floor and walls of the cave, taking nothing for granted, but came up empty handed. After searching for more than an hour, they finally decided to head back down the mountain, disappointed that they didn't find any clues that would lead them to discover the identity of the dead man or why he was killed.

"I'm beyond disappointed," said Rosana. "I was so sure we'd find something. The only thing we saw was what the police already know… the boot prints. And they also said partial finger prints, that's all."

"I'm just as frustrated as you are," said Milena. "I don't get it. Criminals are usually sloppy. Whoever killed this guy must have been a professional. He left nothing behind but his boot prints. He probably wasn't even aware that he left finger prints, but he did. Hopefully, that's enough for an identification of the killer."

On their way down the mountain, Rosana had an idea. "I think we should investigate the west side of the mountain because Steve mentioned that may be the direction John Doe probably came from, and it makes a lot of sense to me because the dogs didn't bark. Also, I doubt he came up from the north end of the mountain because though it's drivable, it doesn't go past the cave and it would take longer to get to it. Plus, a car on the road stands out more than a person would. I'm sure he wouldn't have wanted to draw attention to himself if he was up to no good."

"Good idea." Said Milena as she raised her eyebrows at the prospect of finding a possible clue on the west side of the mountain.

"We can come back tomorrow. Bring a sandwich. We'll do a stake out, from behind the rock walls, like they do on TV cop shows," Rosana said smiling.

"A stakeout?" asked Milena. "Why?"

"Because we didn't find any clues in the cave. So, you know how they say that the criminal always comes back to the scene of the crime?" asked Rosana. "Well, maybe the killer will come back thinking he left clues and try to cover his tracks. Remember, he probably doesn't think anyone comes up here that often. So, if we hide, we can identify him to the police. He won't see us from behind the rock wall."

They made their descent down the mountain and stopped to chat with Steve again. He invited them in for some tea. They sat in the kitchen and enjoyed the chamomile tea that he brewed and the cookies he baked.

"I didn't know you can bake, Steve," said Milena. "My mom bakes pastries and sells them at the farmers' market. You guys should get together and open a bakery."

"Oh, I don't know about that. I'm not that good of a baker, and besides, I like my life just the way it is, no complications," Steve replied with a big grin on his face. "I cook for myself and my dogs. I also hunt with my dogs. So, my days are simple and satisfying. Just the way I like it."

From the kitchen, Rosana could see into the living room. It had lots of bookshelves filled with books. "I noticed you have an extensive library of books," said Rosana. "I love to read. Who is your favorite author?"

"I like Robert Ludlum, Tom Clancy, and Brad Thor. I think their novels are exciting and woven with threads of truth. You just don't necessarily know which of the events are fact or fiction," replied Steve.

"Well, your bookshelves certainly are well organized and contain a wide variety of different subject matter. Your home is well organized too. You've got great taste, Steve, and you did a fabulous job with the renovations," said Milena smiling.

"Thank you; I try. It's not fancy, but it's functional."

"But why don't you have a phone?" asked Milena. "If you don't mind me asking."

"I have a ham radio. Come and see," he said as they got up from the table and walked into the living room. There in a corner nook was a two-tiered desk with his ham radio setup. He showed them the antenna tuner, power amplifier, VHF transceiver, low band transceiver, 2-meter FM transceiver, antenna positioner, and even a telex messaging system with an LCD screen and a keyboard. He also showed them the mic, which was on a stand of its own, so he could talk hands free, and the headset that he sometimes used. "Everything I need is right here," he said with a big smile.

"WOW, that's impressive," said Milena. "But what about your friends? How do you call them?"

"My friends have ham radios. Really, that's all I need. I'm not one for having hour long telephone conversations," he said chuckling.

Though Steve's house was small, it was neat and clean. He never allowed his dogs inside the house. The dogs had their own house in a fenced in area, and they enjoyed Steve's company whenever they were with him whether it was hunting or playing around the compound. Not allowing animals into the house was the rule of thumb on the island. Dogs were treated as animals that had a job or served a function, and not as pets. Steve's dogs had both responsibilities. They were his early warning system of anyone approaching the compound and also helped Steve hunt. On the island, dogs were always kept outside. In the cities, however, dogs were considered pets and they were allowed in the house just like a member of the human family.

Steve had simple, but functional furniture made of wood. His sofa had wood arms and legs, but the overstuffed cushions were made of fabric and looked comfortable. He had blinds on the windows, but no curtains. His fridge was an apartment sized fridge, but he did have a large separate freezer to store the meat from the game he hunted.

"Steve, I'll be right back," said Rosana. I need to use your bathroom."

"Sure, that's fine," replied Steve. "It's in the bedroom."

Because the ancient houses were small and there was no plumbing in the houses, people from centuries past either used their barns or outhouses for toilets. But now, most of the houses all had electricity and plumbing. But Steve's house did not have a bathroom when he purchased it. For that reason, Steve installed an upflush toilet in the bedroom. Doing so saved him from having to build-on to the house to accommodate the toilet. It also saved him from having to install additional plumbing.

After chatting a bit further, the girls bid Steve goodbye, and continued on their way down the mountain and to their respective homes.

The following day the girls headed back up the mountain, past the cave and down the other side. It was a much shorter route than to walk all the way around the mountain to get to the west side of it. The west side of the mountain was lusher than the east side of the mountain. It wasn't as rocky and it fell away at a gentler slope than the east side, which made it easier to walk down. They headed down the mountain very slowly looking for clues such as newly broken twigs off of bushes and large boot prints. Along the way, they passed chest high rock walls that the farmers used to mark off their pieces of properties. The farmers used the rocks and stones that were readily available on the mountain and they piled them up one on top of the other to build the wall. They did this on all sides of the property, leaving a very wide entrance so that they could bring any tilling or harvesting equipment needed into the lot. Even though they used only rocks and no mortar; the walls were sturdy enough that they could safely support multiple people walking on top of the wall, if needed, and sometimes it was needed because the bramble was so thick in places that you couldn't walk any further. So, you got on top of the wall to continue your walk. Looking down at them from the mountain, they looked like a maze of cubicles that you'd find in a place of business.

They made their way into some of the walled off lots, one by one. Some had olive trees growing inside the lot while others had a variety of crops. Some of the larger pieces of land had vineyards growing in them while others had nothing but bramble, but the majority of the lots were barren with only rocks, grass and weeds. Since the rock walls were chest high, the girls were able to see over the rocks for anyone approaching from the west side, and of course, they could see the lush scenery below. They could partially see the Italian alps from up there because the sky was so clear. After about two hours of roaming the mountainside looking for clues and not finding any; they decided to go back up to the top of the mountain to have their lunch and to get a better panoramic view of the islands. They found a shade tree under which they sat to eat their lunch.

"What are you eating?" asked Milena.

"Just some mortadella and cheese. How about you?" asked Rosana.

"Some Genoa salami and cheese," replied Milena. "I also brought some sok to drink. There's plenty for both of us."

"What did you think of Steve's ham radio setup?" asked Rosana. "I knew he had one but I didn't realize how elaborate it was."

"Yes, from what I understand, that antenna he has is a dipole antenna. He can even get international wave lengths on that thing," commented Milena. "At 80-meter wave lengths, he could actually talk to the U.S. from his house."

"Wow, that's amazing," said Rosana. "You know, this whole murder thing is very frustrating. I hope the police call in a more qualified homicide detective. Neither Hrenek nor Radic are really qualified to carry on this type of investigation."

"Oh, I agree," said Milena nodding her head. "They are in over their heads, for sure."

"That's one of the reasons I'm hoping we can solve this murder case. It would really show how inept these two cops really are."

From their vantage point, they could see some of the other islands staggered alongside the coast like pearls cast onto a deep blue velvet sea. To the east, they could see the mainland cities of St. Fillip and Jakov, and Biograd. They could clearly see Galešnjak Island, also known as Lover's Island, which is a natural heart shaped island right off the coast of Pasman Island. The Dalmatian coast actually consists of over 1,200 islands.

There were very few houses on the west side of the mountain and the houses that were there all had solar energy panels either on their roofs or in the fields next to their house. All the houses on the island were located by the seaside. There were no houses on the mountain. For the houses on the west side of the mountain, solar power was their only source of energy as there were no electric power lines on that side of the island. In winter they had fireplaces to keep them warm, but winters on that part of the Dalmatian coast were typically mild, though they have been known to have bouts of frigid days.

After they ate their sandwiches, they decided to descend the mountain on the east side in order to get back to the cave, as they had no luck finding any trace of a clue on the west side of the mountain.

They reached the cave, and with flashlights in hand, they entered the main chamber where the statue of the friar was; and where they found the dead body. By this time, most of the stench had dissipated, though they could still smell it ever so slightly. Once again, they started to comb the floor and walls of the cave, including behind rocks and boulders, but again found nothing.

"We haven't been back there into the depths of the cavern," said Milena.

So, they headed toward the back of the cave to a series of chambers and tunnels. One of the chambers had a hole in the roof where you could see the sky. Pigeons were known to gather there as did bats.

"I know your dad likes to hunt," said Rosana. "Has your dad ever brought home any of the pigeons?"

"I know some of the locals like squab and they hunt them as they fly out of the hole, but my dad never did bring any of them home. He prefers the pheasants. He's brought home pheasant on a number of occasions."

Squab are young pigeons that taste like chicken dark meat and are eaten as a delicacy in many parts of the world. They're very different from city pigeons.

"Be careful of the bats," said Milena. "They scare the crap out of me."

Just as she finished saying that, a bat flew directly toward them. Milena felt the flicker of the bat's wing against her head. Both girls let out a scream that echoed through the chamber. Their scream triggered more bats to swarm from their resting spots. The girls ducked to avoid the avalanche of bats, and in doing so, Rosana slipped and fell on her butt right into the bat feces.

"Yuk," she said in disgust. "Why is it always me that get into this crap?" she said with her nose turned up and not knowing how to get the feces off her clothes.

"Rub your butt up against the wall there," said Milena laughing.

"It's not funny," said Rosana as she brushed her butt up against the wall.

"Oh yes, it is," said Milena still laughing. "I'm really not at all sure we should go down those tunnels," she continued. "I think that's where most of the bats hang out."

"Oh, come on, we need to check everything out," said Rosana. "We'll just have to be quiet when walking through there."

The tunnels were longer and narrower than Rosana thought, and she wasn't at all comfortable walking through them because she started to feel claustrophobic. When the tunnels got too small to walk through, she suggested they turn around and go back. Milena was only too happy to oblige. She didn't want to go down the dank and dirty tunnels in the first place.

After an hour of combing through the chambers and tunnels, they found no clues.

"Well, let's head back to the village," said Milena. "This is very disappointing. It's as if this man was a ghost who just floated into the cave. There's no clues here as to who he was, why he was here, or why he was murdered."

"I know," said Rosana. "It's frustrating."

They headed down the mountain and went about their business in the village for the next few of days. When the weekend came, they decided to go back up to the cave to investigate some more. They were both frustrated that they didn't find anything and thought they may have missed something.

When they got to the entrance of the cave, they were surprised to see a light inside. They both stopped abruptly at the cave entrance.

"Who do you suppose that is?" ask Milena.

"I don't know. Maybe the police?" asked Rosana.

"Or maybe the killer!" said Milena with her eyes wild open and brows raised. "This may be our chance to solve the murder."

"Geez, Milena. I hope it's NOT the killer. Now I'm not sure we should go in," said Rosana a little apprehensive about entering the cave.

"I was kidding. I don't really think it's the killer," said Milena regretting that she even said it might be the killer.

They decided to go in. They turned on their flashlights and cautiously headed toward the moving light. There by the statue was a man with a flashlight milling around as if looking for something.

"Hi, isn't the friar statue interesting?" asked Milena.

The man jumped when he heard Milena's voice, and he turned on his heels as if ready to defend himself. He wasn't expecting anyone to come into the cave.

'Good thing that flashlight isn't a gun,' thought Rosana. *'Wonder why he is so jumpy.'*

"Oh, hi. I'm sorry. I don't speak Croatian," he said in German.

"Do you speak English?" asked Rosana in English.

"Oh yes, I do," he replied smiling.

"That's great," said Rosana in English. "We both speak English."

"Oh, so I see. That's great," said the man smiling at them.

"So," said Milena, "I'll ask you in English. Isn't the friar statue interesting?"

"Oh yes," said the man. "I was just checking it out. It's fascinating. But I noticed what looks like blood on the floor here. Do you know what that's all about?" he asked innocently.
"Yes," said Milena. "Apparently, a man was murdered here. We don't know who he was or why he was murdered."

"WOW! A murder, huh?" said the man. "And who found him?"

"It was our misfortune to find him," said Rosana. "I wish we hadn't."

"Oh? And why is that?" asked the man.

"Because now the police think that we had something to do with his murder," answered Rosana.

"Oh … I see. So, they are making your life miserable, huh?" asked the man. "I can understand why you wish you wouldn't have found the body."

"Are you visiting the island as a tourist or do you have relatives here?" asked Milena.

"Yes, I'm a tourist from uh … from the Netherlands," replied the man. "I just love Croatia."

"Cool," said Milena. "So, it's not the first time you've visited Croatia then. Where are you staying?"

"Oh … I'm staying at a uh … at a bed and breakfast," replied the man nervously.

"What's your name?" asked Rosana.

"Oh sorry, how rude of me," replied the man. "My name is Alex."

"Hi Alex, I'm Rosana and this is my friend Milena. Where in the Netherlands are you from?" she asked innocently.

"Where am I from? Oh … I'm uh … I'm from Amsterdam," he said nodding his head. "I'm here with some friends on holiday."

"I see," said Rosana. "Welcome to our island."

"What a small world!" exclaimed Milena. "My sister recently accepted a job offer in Amsterdam."

"I'm sure she'll love it there," replied Alex. "The people are very friendly."

"How did you find out about the cave?" asked Rosana.

Alex looked around nervously, flexing the fingers on his left hand as his eyes darted from the girls to the entry of the cave, and then replied, "From a friend who used to live on one of the islands."

They chatted a bit longer and then Alex excused himself.

"It was nice meeting you, but I… umm… should be going. I need to meet my friends for lunch."

"Okay, nice meeting you too," said Milena.

"Take care," said Rosana.

"He's cute," said Milena as she watched him leave.

"Oh, you think every boy is cute," said Rosana. "I think you're just boy crazy," she teased.

"Well," she said, still watching him walk away, "he had a sexy accent and he was cute. He was tall, dark, and handsome. And the way he tossed his jet-black hair out of his baby blue eyes was very sexy. What more can a girl ask for?" asked Milena smiling.

"How about some brains," replied Rosana.

"Why do you say that?" asked Milena with a puzzled look on her face.

"Don't you think he acted a little strange?" asked Rosana. "He said he was with a group of friends on holiday, yet his friends didn't come to the cave with him. He came alone. Plus, he was clearly nervous and, in a hurry to leave. I found that very strange."

"You're right. I didn't think of it that way," said Milena.

"I should have tried to get more information from him," said Rosana. "In any event, let's see what, if anything, we can find."

But again, their investigating yielded no clues as to the corpse they found last week in the cave.

As they walked down the mountain, Rosana saw something from the corner of her eye. It looked like a person peeking out from behind a rock wall.

She stopped and grabbed Milena's arm. "Milena. Look," she said as she pointed to the wall. "Someone is there watching us."

Milena turned quickly to look but saw nothing. "You're seeing things. Are you sure you didn't see a little green man from outer space?" asked Milena laughing.

"Oh, very funny, ha-ha. Okay, well, let's get back into town. All this walking has made me hungry. We can come back tomorrow. Something just doesn't feel right, but I can't put my finger on it," said Rosana.

"I don't know where you put it. How can you eat so much and never gain an ounce?" said Milena

— — —

They had dinner with their parents that night and they both told their parents about the stranger they met in the cave. Rosana's father didn't want Rosana to go back to the cave until the police figured out what was going on. He put down his fork, folded his hands, put them on the table and looked at her with piercing eyes as if he was going to chew her out. Rosana knew how to read the signs when her father was angry. She dreaded what was coming. Her stomach tightened right along with her jaw line. She griped the edge of the table top with her left hand and got ready to push away from the table with her right, if need be.

"Damn it, Rosana, didn't I tell you to stay away from that cave until this murder thing is solved?" yelled her father. "And now you tell me there was a man hiding up by the rock walls. You are really asking for trouble. I forbid you to go up there! If I find out you've been back there, you'll have a very sore butt. You hear me?"

But Rosana, being the rebellious adventurer that she was, decided to ignore her father's cautions. *'He won't find out,'* she thought.

"Marko, stop yelling. The neighbors will hear you," said Ana defending her daughter.

But later, when Marko was out of the house and out of ear shot, Ana had a heart to heart with her daughter. They sat at the kitchen table across from each other.

"Rosana," said her mother, "what happened today with that stranger is serious. You shouldn't have gone into the cave if someone was in there. I really think you should listen to your father. You know how he worries. Please, don't go to the cave again until the police figure out who killed that poor man."

"Mom, those cops aren't qualified to solve this murder. You know that too. If you don't want me to go to the cave, why don't you speak to the police chief and tell him he needs to call in a seasoned detective?" said Rosana. "If Milena and I don't solve it, it will never be solved."

"Now honey, that's not true," said her mother. "They will solve it and if they don't, I'm sure the police chief will call in someone who will."

Rosana saw she wasn't going to win this argument, so she stopped talking. She waited until her parents went to bed and then tip-toed down stairs and telephoned Milena. She told Milena to meet her at the village square at 9 o'clock in the morning.

The next day, she and Milena met at the square.

"Did your parents try to stop you from going up to the cave like mine did?" asked Rosana.

"No, but they did say I needed to be careful," said Milena. "Your parents are too strict Rosana. You know how they worry about everything."

"I know. That's what happens when you're an only child. You'd think I was five years old the way he treats me. But I don't care. Pretty soon he'll leave again for his job and I won't see him for months, maybe years, if I'm lucky," said Rosana in an annoyed tone. "But you know what?" she continued. "I brought us some better flashlights. These are the type you can hang from your pants belt and they are so much brighter than the ones we have been using."

"Wow, that's great. Thanks," said Milena.

As they started their walk up the mountain, Milena was the first to speak.

"What are we missing?" asked Milena with her eyebrows furled. "A murder happened here, yet we can't find any clues or evidence as to what happened."

"I don't know," said Rosana, "but my gut tells me that Alex wasn't here as a tourist."

After getting to the cave, they decided to go check out the back chambers again. They searched for a while, but again came up empty handed. Just as they were leaving the back chamber and making their way to the main chamber, they heard someone entering the main chamber.

"Turn off your flashlight," whispered Milena. "I'll bet it's that Alex guy again."

Rosana did so immediately and held onto Milena as they crouched behind a large boulder to hide. Through the distant dim lights of the approaching flashlights, they could see three men walking in, one of which was Alex. They couldn't make out the features of the other two men walking behind Alex.

"The stuff has to be here somewhere," Alex said. "I don't know where he would have hidden it, but it's got to be here. Spread out and search every nook of this place. Also, look for signs of digging. He may have buried it. Pete, you go to the back of the cavern and work your way forward. I'll start here and work toward the back chambers. Joe, you're the skinniest so you go down the tunnels and see where they lead to."

Rosana panicked. *'What if they find us here hiding?'* she thought. *'Oh God, what if my father finds out I'm here?'*

The thought of being discovered by the three men, or that she disobeyed her father, sent her into a frenzy. She started to sweat and to breath hard. Her heart beat faster and faster until she thought it would jump into her mouth. Her insides felt like a lightning bolt hit her. She didn't know what to do, but all she wanted was to get out of the cave… NOW.

She tugged on Milena's shirt and motioned toward the cave entrance to indicate that they should make a run for it.

Milena shook her head to say 'no'. But Rosana just tugged harder on Milena's shirt as Milena again shook her head. Now, Rosana was struck with the fight or flight instinct and stood up to try to make a run for the entrance. Just then Pete turned his flashlight toward the back cavern as he was getting ready to enter it in order to search it. The beam from the flashlight swept over to where the girls were hiding. Rosana slumped into a heap on the floor, but too late. Pete's flashlight had already spotted her. Pete flinched at the sight of someone there. His heart jumped and he took an offensive position ready to fight whoever was hiding there.

"Hey, why are you hiding over there?" came Pete's voice. With that, Alex came running to the back chamber. When he saw the girls, his back straightened and he was nodding his head with a sarcastic knowing half grin on his face.

"I knew it. They know something," said Alex as he quickly came toward the girls and stood in front of them.

"Oh, hi Alex," said Milena nonchalantly. "Fancy meeting you here again today."

"Okay, where have you hidden it?" demanded Alex.

"I don't know what you're talking about," said Milena while trying to appear calm.

"Don't give me that innocent bull shit," said Alex now angered at the cat and mouse game Milena seemed to be playing.

"Honestly, I don't know what you think we hid, but we didn't do anything. We're just a couple of local girls who come up to the cave to get away from the mind-numbing people of the village," she stated as her voice started to faulter.

"Then why were you hiding if you're so innocent?" asked Alex. "No, you know something, so unless you tell me where you hid the stuff, you're coming with us."

"Please! I told you the truth. Neither one of us has any idea what you are talking about," pleaded Milena, now starting to shake with fear. She knew Alex wasn't that nice person that she met in the cave last time. This was a different Alex. A mean and no-nonsense Alex ready to do whatever he needed to get what he wanted. This made both girls very nervous. Their stomachs were doing flips and they both felt like the air was getting too thin in the cave because it was getting harder for them to breath. Of course, the air wasn't getting thinner, it was just their fear that made their throats tighten. Their heads were spinning and all they could think about was making a run for it.

"No! I'm tired of your cat and mouse games!" yelled Alex, "I'm taking you hostage until you divulge where you hid the stuff."

"What stuff!?" blurted out Rosana. "She's telling the truth! We don't know anything about any stuff that you think we hid."

Joe pulled Alex aside and whispered into his ear. "They're just a couple of local stupid teens. I doubt they know anything about what happened. Why would they? Mario wouldn't have had them as accomplices. They are just a couple of dumb teens. Let them go."

"I can't let them go now," said Alex very annoyed. "They know too much already. They will come with us as our hostages."

"Hostages? For what, Alex?"

"Don't you understand, Joe? We can't let them go now until we find the stuff," replied Alex clearly agitated.

"Look, man! You are making this worse than it needs to be. Let them go, man," pleaded Joe.

With that, Alex pushed Joe away and headed toward the girls. Milena, who was normally calm, had a worried look on her face. Her normally pretty eyes were wide open with fright, and there were beads of perspiration gathering on her forehead. She was struck with fear to the point where she felt sick to her stomach and contemplated making a run for the entry of the cave, but then stopped as she saw the hand gun Alex was holding. He pulled it out of his jacket pocket and pointed it at the girls while motioning with it for them to move toward the front of the cave, making sure they saw the gun waving.

Rosana's head was spinning and she felt weak at the knees. All she could think about was making a run of it, and how her father was going to beat her once he found out what happened. She was so upset; she couldn't think straight. Her eyes darted back and forth between Alex's gun and the cave entry. Meanwhile she was getting nauseated from the stress of feeling like a trapped animal.

'Oh my God,' thought Rosana. *'What if they kill us?'*

Alex grabbed Rosana by the arm and yanked her so hard that she let out a scream that echoed throughout the cavern. Then Alex told Joe to take Milena. By this time, Milena was like a deer in headlights frozen in place.

"Don't make me do something I'll regret. Do as I say … MOVE!" yelled Joe to Milena, as he yanked her out of her stance.

"You're coming with us, and if you scream or yell out, or do anything stupid, I'll kill you. I swear it," said Alex pointing a gun at them with snarled lips and an angry glare in his eyes. "Understand?" It was more of a command than a question. Then he motioned to Pete to get behind them, just in case they tried anything stupid, like running away.

The girls were too scared to do anything except what they were told, and Rosana's middle section and chest were heaving up and down from trying to hold back the tears.

They all walked down the west side of the mountain with Alex gripping Rosana's upper arm with his left hand while Joe was grasping Milena's. Both were holding guns in their right hand pointed at the girls. Pete brought up the rear. He too had a gun, just in case one of the girls tried to escape. When they got to the bottom, the men took the girls to a parked black van at the foot of the mountain. Alex slid the van door open on its tracks, and told them to sit in the back. As soon as the van door opened,

Rosana backed away from the van and started twisting her arm back and forth in an attempt to get free.

"Rosana," yelled out Milena in Croatian, "don't run … they'll shoot you."

This stopped Rosana in her tracks. Her heart was beating very fast and she couldn't think. With that, Alex pushed Rosanna into the back of the van. Now he was angry. He agitatedly tied her hands together in back of her with a piece of rope. Rosana hated the feel of the rope. It was prickly and it was too tight. She was so upset at her predicament that she started to cry. Milena didn't get the same rough treatment from Joe, but he did tie her hands in back of her with the rope. Pete sat in the back of the van with the girls pointing a gun at them while Alex and Joe sat in the front discussing their next move. Alex was unmistakably in charge. He told Pete to guard the girls while he and Joe went back into the cave to finish what they started. Before they left, they grabbed six tote bags. Rosana assumed it was for carrying whatever it was they were looking for.

After Alex and Joe left, the girls got a good look at the interior of the van. There were food wrappers and empty water bottles thrown onto the floor of the van, and there was a curled-up rope on top of a black tarp. The tarp looked like it had 3 rectangular items under it. They were about the size of a suitcase, so the girls figured that it must be suitcases.

As they waited for Alex and Joe to come back, Milena and Rosana talked in Croatian to each other.

"These men are going to kill us," said Rosana.

"That's okay, then your father won't have to," said Milena trying to lighten the mood.

"Damn it, Milena!" cried out Rosana. "This is serious. Stop joking around. How are we going to get out of this?"

"They won't kill us, Rosana. They think we know something we don't. If they kill us, they'll never know what it is that we supposedly know," said Milena.

"Okay you two. Stop talking or I'll gag you," said Pete, in a heavy German accent, annoyed that he couldn't understand what they were saying.

As they waited for what seemed like an eternity, all Rosana could think about was how her father would react. There was no way she could think of to get out of this one.

'He is going to kill me. Even if they let us go, I can't go back home again. He'll kill me,' she thought

Milena saw the worried look on Rosana's face. She wished there was something she could do to ease Rosana's mind.

"Pete, do you think we can get a drink of water," asked Milena in an effort to distract Rosana from her thoughts.

"No, we don't have any more water here in the van. You'll have to wait until we get to the campsite," said Pete.

"Campsite?" asked Milena. "I thought you guys were staying in a bed and breakfast."

"Shut up!" yelled Pete. "What! You think we're taking you to a luxury resort or something?" he asked in a mocking tone. "Just sit there and stop talking," he ordered.

A few hours later, they saw Alex and Joe approaching the van empty handed. They sat in the front arguing, but neither Rosana nor Milena could understand exactly what they were arguing about because they were speaking German.

"Alex, I gotta tell you that the only thing you are accomplishing by holding those teens hostage is to put us at a huge risk. You have to let them go," pleaded Joe while also talking with his hands as many Italians do.

"Shut up, Joe!" yelled Alex. "You damn well know what's at stake. If we don't find the stuff, we will be killed. Is that what you want? Are you that ready to give up? Besides, it's too late now. They already know what we look like, so just shut your trap!"

Milena and Rosana looked at each other wide eyed and terri-fied. Though they didn't understand German, they could tell by the tone of the voices that the two men were at odds with each other, and that wasn't good for them. Their hands shook and they were desperate and feeling hopeless as there was nothing they could do to get out of their situation. Rosana was almost in tears and Milena was talking to her in Croatian trying to calm her down.

"My heart is racing, I feel sick to my stomach, and my hands are shaking. You know I have a weak heart due to Afib, and I'm scared they will kill us just like they did that other guy," cried Rosana.

"I'm not feeling much better myself, but you can't let them see that you're scared," replied Milena. "Otherwise, they will just continue to intimidate us, and you certainly can't afford to put any more stress on your heart. So, please think about something you love… like being on top of the mountain."

"Shut-up you two," commanded Pete again.

After a few minutes of arguing with Joe, Alex started the car and they drove a short distance to a camp site. When they arrived, they escorted the girls out of the van and told them to sit under a nearby tree. The campsite was set up with one tent and a firepit stacked with wood ready for when needed. It was located in an area where there were many trees, as the trees gave them cover from prying eyes.

With their hands still tied in back of them, Pete sat the girls with their backs to the tree and tied a rope around their waists and chests and the tree to keep them in place. He also tied up their feet so they couldn't run away. This was too much for Milena who hated being restrained. She was twisting and turning trying to get herself loose, but to no avail.

"You'd better stop fidgeting, if you don't want me to punch your lights out," said Pete with his eyes scrunched together and his lips pierced in a straight line, which made him look very mean. Milena decided she'd better do as he said.

When night fall came, Joe started a fire and cooked some sausages over the fire. The sausages were pierced through the middle with a skewer that Joe had whittled out of a stick he found nearby. They also had a loaf of store-bought bread onto which Joe placed the cooked sausage to make a sandwich. There were enough for all five of them. The girls' hands were untied long enough for them to eat their sandwich and then tied back up again. The men talked amongst themselves in German. The girls took advantage of this and whispered to each other in Croatian.

"What are we going to do Milena? I'm telling you; these men are desperate and dangerous. I don't know what I was thinking coming up to the cave. My father is right. I AM STUPID!" said Rosana crying.

"Stop crying. They won't kill us. But I don't like this. Why haven't they questioned us further and why are they ignoring us if we are their only hope of finding whatever they're looking for. It's like they are waiting for someone to join them or something," said Milena.

"Maybe they are waiting for the guy that tortures people to get us to talk," said Rosana through her tears in a quivering voice.

Now the men were turning around to look at the girls as if they were talking about them. That scared them both as they didn't know what to expect. So they just stared back wild eyed and frightened.

"Stop talking!" yelled Alex. That's all he said. So the girls did as he asked.

Later, Alex and Pete went to sleep in the tent while Joe took his turn in keeping an eye on the girls outside by the old olive tree to which they were tied. Being that the other two men were asleep, Rosana saw this as an opportunity to talk to Joe to see if he would untie her.

"I have to go to the bathroom," said Rosana.

"So do I," echoed Milena.

Joe looked puzzled. He crooked his neck to the left and then to the right as if trying to figure out what to do next. Then he figured if he let them go one at a time it would be okay as he could control the situation.

"Okay," he said. "I'll untie you, one at a time; but I'm telling you now, no funny business."

First, he untied Rosana and led her to a tall and overgrown area to let her relieve herself.

"Go here, by this bush," he said.

"What? You're gonna watch me pee?" Rosana asked.

With that, Joe turned away and kept his eye on Milena. After a few minutes, with his back still facing Rosana, he said to her, "Hey, come on, what's keeping you?" He kept his voice low as not to wake the other two men, but there was no answer. He repeated the whisper a little louder, figuring that Rosana didn't hear him the first time, but still no answer.

Annoyed, he walked behind the bush to see what was happening. He disappeared behind the bush, and seconds later Milena heard a loud yelp from the man. Rosana came running toward Milena from behind the bush and feverishly proceeded to untie her. She was trembling all over and her hands were shaking so much that she was fumbling and having a hard time trying to untie her friend.

"What happened?" asked Milena.

"I…I…found a l…large rock and… umm… I…ah…hit him over the head with it," shuddered Rosana trembling with fear.

"Oh my God," replied Milena. "You didn't kill him, did you?" whispered Milena with darting glances from the tent to the bush to be sure none of the men were awake to deter the girls from their getaway.

"Ohh, I doubt it. I think I… ah… I think… I…ah… I… I just knocked him out," replied Rosana, unable to even think clearly from the fright that overtook her.

They grabbed the flashlights that were laying on the ground next to the tree and ran as fast as they could. They couldn't see very far in the dark even with the light of the flashlights. This added to their near hysteria as they suspected Joe would come to and the men would come after them.

As they ran, they kept tripping over rocks and falling in their frenzied panic to get away. They couldn't even talk they were so worked up.

"Rosana, slow d-d-d-down," pleaded Milena She was so frazzled that she was stuttering her words. "We c-c-c-can't see very far and we're lucky we d-d-d-ddon't sprain our ankles. We're all scraped up from the underbrush."

"I don't care. I just want to get away from this place." Rosana replied through tears.

As they continued running, they kept tripping and falling.

They went up the mountain, over the top and down the other side. By that time, they were both panting pretty hard, half from running up the mountain and half out of fear. They kept running until they heard the dogs barking from Steve's compound. They were never so relieved to hear those dogs barking.

When Steve heard the dogs, he immediately came outside because the dogs didn't normally bark at night. As the girls got closer to the compound, Steve realized it was them. Steve was alarmed at the sight of them as they looked bloody, disheveled and terrified. He had never seen the girls come up to the compound at night and certainly not in this terrified state. He realized that something was terribly, terribly wrong. He opened his arms and the girls ran to him and broke down crying, one on each shoulder. Steve led the girls into the house and he told them to sit down while he went to retrieve his first aid kit.

As soon as they entered the house, Milena yelled, "BOLT THE DOOR!" Steve quickly bolted the door, got his rifle, and loaded it with bullets. He was ready for whoever came to the door. He cleaned off their knees and elbows while they were talking over each other trying to tell him what happened. He made some tea to calm them down. Steve himself was frazzled as he didn't know what was going on and he'd never seen the girls in this state of distress.

"Now calmly tell me what happened," he said. "I couldn't understand anything you were saying as you were both talking at the same time. Now, ONE at a time, tell me."

Again, the girls both began talking at the same time. They were tripping over their words because they were talking so fast and furious.

"Wait, wait," said Steve. "I can't understand a single word you're saying because you're still talking over each other. Milena, tell me slowly, what happened."

Milena started to tell Steve what happened.

"We were in the cave when we heard someone coming and saw flashlights. We were so scared. I thought I was going to die. Then we hid…"

"And then they found us," interjected Rosana. "I was shaking like a leaf and all I could think about was making a run for the cave entrance. Then, they took us hostage."

"Yes, because they thought we know something," said Milena.

"But, we don't." added Rosana. "Then they took us down to the van…" said Rosana.

"At gunpoint!" interjected Milena. "At the bottom of the mountain on the west side to a camp site. But Alex had told us he was staying in a bed and breakfast."

"So he lied, and Pete made fun of us. Then we were tied up to a tree," said Rosana now crying again.

"Like animals. But later, Rosana had a brilliant idea. She told Joe she had to go to the bathroom," interjected Milena.

"Then I hit him over the head with a rock when he came looking for me behind the bush," said Rosana.

"That's how we got away," finished Milena. "But we couldn't see anything in the dark and kept tripping and falling down.

It was as if they were one person telling it. Steve's eyes kept bouncing back and forth between the girls as they told their incredible story. He didn't know what to make of the information the girls were telling him about being tied up and taken hostage. This was bizarre and criminal behavior in any city, but especially on a quiet little-known island like Pasman.

"What an ordeal you went through," he said. "Did they hurt you?"

"No, but we are terrified that they will come after us," said Milena. "They are convinced that we know where whatever they're looking for is hid. I didn't understand what they were saying because they spoke German, but I do know that the stuff they keep referring to must be very valuable."

"This is all very bizarre. These men are strangers on our island. They're up to no good, but we don't know what. They lied to you about where they are staying and then tied you up and took you hostage because they thought you knew something you didn't. WOW! These all sound like desperate measures from desperate men. Whatever it is they are looking for must be worth a fortune. I think we have to call the police," said Steve.

'Yes, they certainly did lie,' thought Rosana. *'What else did they lie about?'*

"Well, it's either money, drugs or jewels. What else can it be?" said Milena. "Maybe they are jewel thieves," she said as her eyes widened and lit up.

"No, it's not money," said Rosana. "They wouldn't refer to money as 'stuff'. It's something else of value."

"We need to call our parents too," said Milena. "They are probably worried sick that we didn't come home tonight. We never stay out this late."

"My father is going to kill me," said Rosana through her tears. "He told me to stay away from the cave."

"Don't worry, Rosana. Sure, he'll be mad at you for a while, but he will get over it," said Steve.

"No, you don't understand, Steve," said Rosana. "He freaked out when I told him we were at the cave yesterday. He told me in no uncertain terms that I wasn't to go up there again. He will kill me for sure when he finds out what happened tonight."

"Don't worry, it will be okay, you'll see," said Steve. "I'm going to take you home. He won't do anything to you with me there."

"Maybe not, but he will give me hell after you leave," said Rosana. She was seriously thinking of running away from home rather than to face her father.

Steve was silent, but he was determined to protect Rosana as best as he could. He walked to the little nook in the living room where his ham radio was setup. He turned it on and tuned it to the police frequency. He spoke to a dispatcher regarding what happened.

"I live up the mountain in Nevidane and my name is Steve Novak. A couple of local girls by the names of Rosana and Milena came frantically to my door because they had just escaped three criminals who had taken them hostage. We think they were somehow involved with the dead body they found in the cave. Yes, the cave. I'm going to be taking them home, but I need you to call the girls' parents to assure them that both girls were unharmed and I will escort them home. This way they wouldn't worry that something would happen to them if they walked home alone without any escort."

Then the dispatcher asked a few questions including the last names of the girls. Steve provided all the information requested and signed off. Then, Steve grabbed a flashlight, his rifle and some ammunition in preparation for the walk down the mountain and to the girls' houses.

Steve, his trusted side kick Butch, and the girls headed down the mountain toward the village. It wasn't easy making their way in the dark with just the light from the flashlights. It was very slow going, but they finally made it down into the village without incident. As promised, Steve escorted each of the girls to their respective homes safely. First, he escorted Milena home as her house was closer. When her parents opened the door, they rushed to hug and kiss her.

"Steve, we owe you a debt of gratitude for bringing our daughter back safe and sound. Thank you so much Steve," said Angelo. "Won't you come in for a cup of coffee?"

"Thank you, but no. I need to get Rosana home," said Steve. "I was happy to do it. These poor, brave girls went through a lot and I'm just glad they were able to escape before something terrible happened. You have a good night now," said Steve.

Then, Steve and Rosana walked to Rosana's house. Steve noticed how worried Rosana looked.

"Rosana, it will be alright. I'm here and your father won't hit you while I'm there," he said.

"You don't know him, Steve. He is a hot head. He flies off the handle so quickly. I wish he wasn't home. I wish he was at sea," said Rosana biting her lower lip and shaking out her fingers to relieve some of the stress.

Upon arriving at Rosana's house, they didn't even have to knock because the door flung open and Marko was standing in the doorway with Ana slightly behind him.

"What the hell did you get yourself into this time?" he demanded. "Look at you! You're a mess," said her father lashing out at her. "And that dog can't come inside," he directed his comment to Steve. Steve gave Butch the command to 'stay' and then walked into the house.

As they stepped inside, Marko slammed the door behind them.

"Didn't I tell you not to go up to the cave?" he asked in a harsh tone. "What the hell were you thinking? Didn't I tell you not to go back to the cave until this murder thing was solved? You stupid, stupid girl," he shouted. "You could have been killed," he said as he suddenly, without any warning, back handed her across the face. Rosana let out a cry from the pain.

Steve immediately flew to Marko's side and looked on in shock, debating if he should deck Marko or not. He couldn't believe the man could be so cruel to his daughter who was visibly shaken to the core. But he knew that the people of the village were the type who got highly offended if a neighbor interfered with how parents raised their children. He'd heard it before, "Don't tell me how to raise my child." So he bit his tongue.

"Marko!" yelled Ana. "Stop that! Can't you see she is distraught?"

But Marko ignored his wife and continued, "You'll never amount to anything because you're so stupid and you don't listen."

As he said that, he lifted his hand to slap his daughter again. But this time, Steve stepped forward and grabbed his hand in midair. Rosana was relieved that Steve interceded on her behalf. No one had ever done that before, except her poor mother who sometimes took the brunt of his brutality when defending Rosana.

As much as Steve knew the unwritten rule of not interfering with how people raise their children, he couldn't just stand there and let Marko hit his daughter again.

"Marko, stop!" said Steve in a forceful voice. "Your daughter is far from stupid! She is very clever and very brave. She kept her wits about her and was the reason the girls escaped. She was resourceful when she grabbed the rock and hit one of her captors over the head with it. Give the girl some credit, will you?" he said with steely eyes focused like rays into Marko's. With that Marko backed off and calmed down as bullies usually do when confronted, especially since Steve towered over him. Then he sat down in a chair and he wiped his forehead with the back of his hand. He sat there in the chair staring at the floor. It was unclear as to whether he was worried sick over what might have happened to his daughter, or if he was embarrassed at his behavior… maybe both.

"Jesus, do you know what she put us through?" he asked Steve rather loudly. "We were worried sick because of the murder. She shouldn't have been up there. I warned her to stay away, but she never listens," said Marko now turning his head and looking at his daughter with grave concern.

"Marko, did you listen to your father when you were her age? Look at it this way. We now know what the guys look like thanks to the girls and they are safe," said Steve. "They can give the police a detailed description of the men which will greatly increase the odds of them finding these criminals. The girls even know where their camp site is and what their car looks like."

"You're right," admitted Marko, much to Steve's surprise because Marko never gave credit to anyone and never admitted he was wrong. "But I insist that I be present when the police question my daughter."

- 4 -

THE DISCOVERY

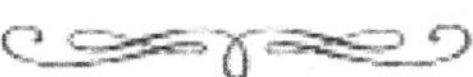

Early the next day, the police called Milena's and Rosana's parents and told them they wanted to ask the girls some questions about the events that took place in the cave and about being taken hostage. They also radioed Steve. They all agreed to meet at the police station in Preko.

When they arrived at the police station, Marko spoke to the officer at the front desk and told him Officer Hrenek was expecting them. The officer led them to an interrogation room that had six chairs, a table, and a Croatian flag on the wall, along with a couple of benches up against the opposite wall. Over the benches was what looked like a large mirror, but everyone knew it was a two-way mirror for when they did interrogations. The officer told them that Officer Hrenek would be with them in a couple of minutes, and then he left. The men and the girls sat behind the table while Mira and Ana sat on a bench. Officers Hrenek and Radic entered the room a few minutes later.

After the usual pleasantries, the girls gave the officers a detailed description of what the three men looked like, the description of the car, and the license plate number of the car.

"Alex and Joe were about the same height and weight. Medium height, maybe 5'8" and average build, probably around 150

81

- 160 pounds. Pete was taller, maybe about 5' 10" and much slimmer, like a string bean. I'd guess about 140 pounds," said Milena.

"The head guy was Alex and he had an accent, and said he was from Amsterdam," said Rosana. "He had jet black hair and baby blue eyes. Joe was the one who wanted to let us go, and he had an Italian accent. He had black hair and hazel eyes with a mole on the left side of his face. He also had a pencil mustache. Pete was the one that was ordered to hold us at gun point. He had mousey colored hair with blue eyes and a pointed nose. But Alex was their leader for sure."

"The good thing about a small island, like Pasman, is that there is only one way off the island—by sea," said Milena. "You must either have a boat or you have to take the ferry to the mainland. If you don't have a boat of your own, you are at the mercy of the sea ferry's timetable."

"They don't have a boat," said Rosana in almost a whisper. She was afraid that whatever she said would implicate her as an accomplice to the murder, but she continued anyway. "As we told you, they had a black van, with the license number we gave you before. Since there are no car rental agencies on the island, they had to have rented the van elsewhere and had to have taken the ferry to the island. They probably drove from Italy, as the license plate was from Italy, down the Dalmatian coast and then took the ferry to the island."

"That's very interesting," said Officer Radic with some excitement in his voice. "I made some inquires and found out that a bank in Amsterdam was robbed. They only had one witness, the bank manager, because it was early in the morning. The bank manager was coming in early to work on some paperwork before the bank opened. The thieves caught him off guard just as he was opening the bank's door to go in. There were three of them and they had on Halloween masks. We have a vague description of them, but that's all. The height and weight of the description matches what you told us about your abductors. I'm betting that the men who abducted you are the bank robbers from Amsterdam. So, they must have been looking for the stolen money."

'*Seriously?*' thought Rosana, '*the height and weight of the bank robbers matches the description we gave you? That describes more than half the men in Europe, you flaming idiots.*'

"We found out the identity of the dead man you found in the cave," said Officer Hrenek. "His name is Mario Martinovic. He was born on the island of Ugljan and he has a police record for theft. That's how we discovered his identity, by the fingerprints. We contacted his parents, on the next island, to see if he'd been in contact with them, but he hadn't. He left the island in his early twenties after a run-in with the law in Zadar. He is estranged from his parents. They haven't heard from him in more than ten years. That coincides with what Alex told you about his friend having lived on one of the islands. We believe that Mario was the driver of the getaway car. We think they split up after the robbery and the driver was supposed to take the money to a safe hiding place to be divided among the four men at a later date. But we believe he fled Amsterdam instead, and came to the island to hide the money here because he intended to keep it all for himself. According to his parents, he knew about the cave because he often came to Pasman to spend time with his cousins who lived here in the village, and he told his parents about going to the cave with his cousins."

"And what a better place to hide the money than in a cave that most people don't visit because they don't know it exists, except of course, for you two," said Officer Radic with contempt in his voice.

"Now, wait a minute," said Steve. "I hope you aren't implying what I think you are implying. Officer Radic. If you think these girls are mixed up in this, you are 100% wrong. Instead of focusing on the girls, you should be doing everything you can to track down these men."

"Now that we have a description of the men, we will dispatch officers to both the Preko and Tkon ferry stations. If they are intending to leave the island by ferry, we will catch them," replied Officer Radic.

'Yeah, right,' thought Rosana, *'they are probably long gone by now. A day late and a dollar short, asshole.'*

The officers thanked everyone for coming into the police station. Officer Hrenek gave Steve his business card and told him to call if he sees anything suspicious in his neck of the woods. The officers told the girls to call them if they thought of anything else.

"Steve, thank you for coming out and for sticking up for our girls," said Angelo. With that, everyone departed and went back to their respective homes.

'Yes, thank you Steve," echoed Marko.

The following day, Milena and Rosana met at the café to discuss what happened yesterday. As they sipped their lemonades, Rosana told Milena that her dad was very angry with her for disobeying him. She described how he smacked her across the face and yelled at her saying she was stupid, and how Steve came to her defense.

"You aren't stupid, Rosana," said Milena. "You know how he is. He blows his top, but when he calms down, he will be sorry he yelled at you and try to seek your forgiveness with some gift, like he always does. I wouldn't worry too much about upsetting him. You did nothing wrong. It wasn't your fault that we got abducted."

"He didn't even give me credit for the quick thinking I did when I got Joe to untie me," said Rosana in a disappointed voice.

"I grabbed the rock and hit him over the head, without thinking. I don't know where the courage came from."

"Well, I'm proud of you," said Milena. "You were very brave and you saved our lives. Who knows what they would have done had it not been for you knocking Joe out like that."

"But I'm afraid that if they find us, they will kill us," said Rosana.

"They won't kill us because they think we know where the money is hidden. Besides, they are probably long gone by now. After we escaped, they must know we went to the police to describe what they looked like. Alex isn't stupid. He kept us hostage because we could identify them to the police. Or maybe, they would first want to find the money because they are convinced that we know where it is… then they'd kill us," she said teasingly while smiling her devilish smile.

"That's not funny, Milena. I'm really scared. And like I said before, it's not money they are looking for. It's something else because they kept saying 'stuff'," said Rosana.

"But the cops said they robbed a bank. What else could they have taken that's in a bank and is valuable?" asked Milena. "Do you think it was jewelry, or loose diamonds, or bonds from someone's safety deposit box?" asked Milena. "But the bank manager didn't say anything about safety deposit boxes," she said answering her own question. "So, what are we going to do? I don't want to walk around looking over my shoulder for the rest of my life."

Rosana didn't say anything because she didn't know what to say. She was more confused than ever. The men were clearly looking for something worth risking their lives for, but what?

"I know this is dangerous, but let's ask Steve to accompany us to the cave," said Milena. "He can bring his dog Butch and his rifle and stand outside the cave just in case the men come back."

"Oh, I don't know about that," said Rosana. "My father will kill me if I go back up there, and we have already been up there a few times. We didn't find anything. Milena, I think we should just lay low."

"No, he won't kill you, not if we have protection. Butch will bark well in advance of seeing anyone come up the mountain and Steve has a rifle. We will be just fine," said Milena. "Let's go talk to Steve to see if he is willing to come up to the cave with us."

They paid for their drinks and left the café. Then, foolishly, and with some trepidation from Rosana, the girls again made their way up the mountain and to Steve's compound. Milena enthusiastically told Steve their plan. He listened to their story with reservations.

"Seems to me that with all the times you've gone to the cave to look for clues, you've had no luck. What makes you think you'll have any luck this time?" Both girls were silent and weren't sure how to reply. Steve continued, "If you're hell bent on going back again, I think you should take a new approach and take a couple of shovels with you to do some digging. I could help you dig. Butch will stay put outside the cave entrance if I tell him to. As you know, he is well trained to obey my commands."

"That's perfect!" said Milena. "Oh Steve, thank you!" she said, grateful that he agreed. "We will be back tomorrow morning, if that's okay with you."

"Yes, that will be fine," said Steve. "I have a few chores to finish today, so tomorrow will be a good day to help you with your search."

— — —

As agreed, the girls arrived at Steve's house early next morning. The three of them made their way up the mountain to the cave, with Butch happily trotting along at Steve's side. Steve's rifle was slung over his shoulder and he carried a small cooler filled with some water bottles. The girls each carried a shovel, and each of them had flashlights hanging from their belts. They were prepared for digging in the cave. Upon arriving at the cave, Steve gave a command to Butch to 'stay' while he and the girls went inside.

The girls started digging in different locations of the cave where they thought they might find the money, or whatever it was that the criminals were so desperately looking for. At the very least, they hoped to find clues to where the 'stuff' was hidden, while Steve explored the cave further in the interior chambers to see if he could spot something the girls may had missed.

Rosana started digging near the friar statue and Milena started digging by a large boulder against the wall of the main chamber. They thrusted their shovels into the cave floor thinking it would be as easy as digging in the fertile fields, but they were wrong. Digging into the cave floor was difficult because of the way the cave was formed. There were lots of rocks under the soil of the cave, and since no rain fell inside the cave, the ground was dry and hard. They had to chip away at the soil to break it up; but they kept at it. They dug for what seemed like hours, with perspiration running down their faces and backs from the difficulty of their digging efforts. In reality, it was only about half an hour. Milena was just about to give up when she suddenly heard a dull thud as her shovel hit the ground. To her, it sounded like she hit metal. All the weariness she was feeling suddenly disappeared and now she was filled with energy to keep going.

"Rosana!" she yelled. "I think I hit something."

The two of them dug frantically in anticipation of discovering a metal chest or some type of clue. However, when they finally exposed the surface of what made the thud, it turned out to be a stone. On the stone, there was some sort of carving. Excitedly, they cleared away the dirt to get a better look. At first, what they saw didn't register and made no sense. There, etched into the stone, was a cross with a strong resemblance to the Knights Templar cross and a carving of a keystone right below it. They looked at each other, baffled. Milena shrugged her shoulders and scrunched her eyebrows together as if to say, '*What the heck is this?*'

Rosana was just as perplexed. Her excitement disappeared and a sad disappointing look took over her face as her shoulders relaxed and her head slumped to her chest in defeat. She was expecting to find a metal chest, not a rock.

"What do you think these symbols mean?" asked Milena. "Could this be the Knights Templar cross?" she asked with wide eyed excitement as she realized that if it was the Knights Templar cross, it was an important clue. "We studied this stuff in school and it looks just like the pictures in our books. Was the stone put there by the ancient Knights Templars and if so, why? And what does this keystone mean?" she continued.

"Do you think this has anything to do with Mario, the dead man?" asked Rosana, perking up.

The more they talked about it the more questions they had. When Steve came back into the main chamber of the cave, they eagerly showed him the stone with the cross and the keystone carved into it. Steve was just as perplexed as the girls.

"A keystone is the wedge-shaped stone normally found at the top of an arch or a vault," explained Steve. "The romans used keystones for arches that were rounded to give the arch stability by redirecting the weight of the arch down and out. And it does look old enough to have been buried there by Romans or Templars centuries ago, but who actually buried it? More importantly, why was it buried here in front of this rock? Is there any significance to where it was buried? What is it trying to tell us?"

"I know what a keystone is," said Milena, "but I don't know what it's trying to tell us, if anything."

"This does look like a Knights Templar cross. I also remember reading about the Knights Templars," said Rosana. "They were once revered Crusaders who actually started the very first bank ever in existence. But Philip IV, king of France, wanted to disgrace and disband the templars in order to confiscate their treasure and land holdings. So, when the king outlawed them for denying Christ and secret devil worship, the Vatican charged them with heresy. They were subjected to an inquisition, torture and death. They were hunted down and thrown into prisons, and their riches were seized. This happened on Friday the 13th. That's why today the number 13, and Friday the 13th, are considered bad luck. However, only 10% of the Knights Templars were caught, or put to death, and the rest of them took action to protect their massive treasures and sacred items. They hid them in castles and in underground vaults and even shipped them to foreign countries. It was reported that there was a fleet of 18 ships belonging to the Knights Templars at a Harbor in France, and on the night before the massacre, they sailed for parts unknown presumably with their treasure. Any treasure and sacred artifacts that they may have had, such as the Holy Grail, the Ark of the Covenant, wood from Jesus' cross, and gold, would have been hidden away. There have even been discoveries of underground Templar caves and secret chambers where they lived and stashed their wealth."

"People still search for those treasures. It's still even romanticized today with movies, such as Indian Jones, The DaVinci

Code, and others," said Milena. They are based on the treasure of the Knights Templar."

The three of them looked at each other dumbfounded, and as if on cue, they turned and stared at the boulder behind them.

"Are you thinking what I'm thinking?" Rosana asked. Without anyone actually answering, they all stood up and started to examine the boulder simultaneously.

They examined all sides of the boulder. The rock was between four and five feet tall. The top and sides of the rock that faced the cave were not flat, so as hard as they tried, it wasn't easy to grab onto it in order to try to budge it. Then, Steve, being the tallest of the three of them, examined the top of the boulder. As he wiped away the dirt from the top of the boulder, markings that looked like scratches in the boulder caught his eye. He excitedly kept wiping the surface because he could see there was actually something carved into it. When he wiped away enough of the dirt, he saw a small carving on the top of the boulder in the shape of a roman keystone.

"Girls," he shouted in his excitement, "I found something," he said in almost a giggle as he realized what he was looking at. Now the girls were getting excited.

"What is it?" asked Milena.

"It looks like a keystone!" said Steve as he burst into laughter, unable to contain his excitement.

"WOW! Now we know for sure the keystone carved on the buried stone and on the boulder are somehow connected," said Milena.

"There might even be a chamber behind this boulder. Come on, let's put some muscle into it," said Steve unable to control his enthusiasm.

Rosana and Milena scrambled to help Steve push the boulder out of the way, but it didn't budge. After pushing on it without any results, they started to pull on it. All three of them pulled and tugged with all their might. To their surprise, as they gave the boulder a good yank, the boulder not only budged, it swung open!

A pintle, which is a pivot pin about 4 to 5 inches in diameter, was exposed on the inside of the boulder's doorway. This is what enabled the boulder to pivot open. The girls' eyes were wild with wonderment. They'd never seen a pintle. Simultaneously, they all shined their flashlights into the arched chamber. Upon walking into the chamber, they felt cobwebs sticking to their faces and clothing, and they started to quickly brush them away.

'Ewww,' said Rosana. "These cobwebs are gross."

At first, it didn't register what they were looking at, but then after they brushed away some of the cobwebs off their faces, what they saw left them speechless. There before them were old, worn-out, and opened wooden treasure chests loaded with jeweled necklaces, tiaras, crowns, and bracelets. Other chests were over-filled with gold coins, while others had gold chalices and silver goblets. Some chests were still closed. The chests were of various sizes, some opened and some closed, but all of them looked ancient.

'Could this be the Knights Templar treasure?' wondered Rosana.

There was so much treasure stashed away in the chamber that much of it was just piled up in batches on the floor of the chamber.

Rosana, Milena, and Steve stood there awe struck, with their mouths open, taking it all in. The magnitude of what they saw was overwhelming and surreal. It was truly a sight of unbelievable proportions.

The room was about 16 feet by 20 feet. The chamber was musty with cobwebs hanging from the ceiling and dead bugs on the floor. In the corner of the chamber was a neatly stacked pile of what appeared to be white bricks taped with brown tape. Still speechless, no one spoke. They were so mesmerized by the sight that they didn't notice the door had swung closed behind them.

"Look at this treasure," Milena said finding her voice again. "Do you think this is part of the Knights Templar's treasure? Ohhhh, do you smell that foul order. My head is spinning and I'm getting nauseated," she continued as she put one hand over her nose and mouth.

"I'm getting lightheaded," said Rosana as she rubbed her irritated eyes.

"This chamber has been closed up for so long that built up hydrogen sulfide gas is making you sick. That's the rotten egg smell that you're smelling now," explained Steve.

"But look at some of these cobwebs," said Rosana also covering her nose and mouth and trying to keep from throwing up. "We aren't the first ones to find this chamber. Someone's been here recently before us. See how the cobwebs are swept away to one side in certain places? And see the foot prints?"

Rosana, being the most curious one of them all, cautiously walked over to what looked like white bricks in the dimly light chamber. Upon further examination, she concluded it might be cocaine because it looked like the cocaine she saw on those narc TV shows.

"Hey, come over here and take a look at this," she beckoned. "What does this look like to you?"

Steve walked over. He pulled out a pocket knife and poked a small hole into the plastic that was wrapped around the brick of white stuff. He stuck his pinky finger into the hole, pulled out a tiny bit of the white powder, and rubbed it on his gums. The taste was bitter and it smelled like gasoline or kerosene, and then his gums went numb. "It's cocaine," he said, unable to believe the words coming out of his mouth.

"Am I the only one who senses there is danger here?" asked Milena.

"Yes, we are in danger in more ways than one," said Steve. "We need to close this up, cover our tracks by filling in those holes you dug in the main chamber, and try to erase any trace of us being here. We need to figure out how to handle this discovery and what it all means. Let's get started NOW. We can discuss this in detail when we get to the compound."

But when they turned around to exit the chamber, they were surprised to see that the door to the chamber had closed behind them.

"Oh my God!" exclaimed Rosana in a panicked tearful voice. "How will we get out of here now?"

"Don't worry," said Steve calmly. "This door pivots out so all we need to do is to push on it, like this," he said as he started to push on the door, but it didn't budge. "Come here and help me push. Put your entire body weight onto it," said Steve.

The girls walked over to where Steve was standing and leaned heavily into the door.

"Now, PUSH," said Steve

With the three of them bearing down on the door, the door slowly swung open.

"Oh thank God," said Rosana, taking a deep breath. As stale as the air was in the main chamber of the cave, it was a delight compared to the air in the vault.

It took them a while to cover their tracks so that it didn't look like it had been disturbed or that anyone was digging in the cave. With their flashlights resting on the floor shining light toward the holes they dug, they frantically filled in the holes. Then they swept the floor with their feet and with shrub branches. When they were finished, they were exhausted with sweat trickling down their backs and foreheads.

They exited the cave, took a deep breath, and began their descent down the mountain, with Butch by their side. Suddenly Butch stopped, jumped around and pointed his nose toward the direction of the rock walls behind them, while barking wildly.

"Why is Butch barking?" asked Rosana.

"I don't know," said Steve. "But you two head back to the compound. I'll go back up to see what's going on."

"Silence!" Steve commanded Butch. Butch immediately stopped barking. Steve, along with Butch, walked back up the mountain. From his vantage point on the mountain, he saw people approaching from the west side. It was the police. Steve stood waiting for them to reach him as he gave Butch the command to 'sit'.

"Steve," said Hrenek, "What are you doing up here?"

"Just walking and enjoying the cooler weather," replied Steve. "What are you doing here? Are there any new developments?"

Without answering him, Hrenek asked, "Steve, have you seen anything suspicious while you were walking around up here?"

"No. What exactly should I have seen?" he asked.

"We received a call and were told that there were three suspicious looking men camped out at the bottom of the mountain, on private property, for a few nights already, and that piqued our interest, as it may be the men who abducted the girls," said Officer Radic.

"You may want to get a search party out here pronto to search the areas behind the rock walls. They make good hiding places," replied Steve hoping that the police and search parties would keep the three men away from the cave for a while until he and the girls figured out their next move.

After they chatted a bit further, the police went on their way and Steve and Butch descended the mountain again. When he got to the compound, he found the girls waiting for him outside his home.

"Who was there? Why was Butch barking?" asked Milena.

"The police were on the west side of the mountain. They were following up on a call about three suspicious looking men camping out at the foot of the mountain," he told them.

"Three men? That means Joe is okay. I didn't give him a fatal blow on the head. But, that's not a good sign," said Rosana with a worried look on her face. "What if they find the secret chamber? Or, worse yet, what if they come looking for us?"

"That's why we need to talk about this now," said Steve. "We need to figure out our next steps and we need to do it fast. Those men could be hiding behind those rock walls. But I don't think they saw us coming out of the cave because Butch didn't bark."

"I agree," said Milena. "He barks relentlessly at the slightest noise."

"Come on inside. I'll make lunch and we can talk while we eat. Do you like tuna fish?" asked Steve.

"Yes, that's fine," answered Milena.

During lunch they discussed how best to handle their find. This was no ordinary treasure that they found. It would make world headlines. They had a ton of questions.

"How are we going to handle that type of responsibility?" asked Rosana.

"What are the rules around finding historic ancient treasure?" asked Milena. "Do we get to keep it, finders' keepers? Does the land owner get to keep it? Who owns the land? The government? Plus, there was a pile of cocaine in the cave. What happens to that?" Her mind was racing with questions.

"I hate to be the bearer of bad news," said Steve, "but that cave is on government land. So, that means we don't get a finder's reward, much less keep any part of it."

"I'm sure that the crooked cops, Radic and Hrenek, know that the cave is on government land," said Rosana. "We can't tell them about the chamber."

They all agreed to keep their secret chamber quiet for now. The girls also thought it best to tell their parents about what they found and to get their opinions of this, or at least Milena did.

"I'm afraid to go home," said Rosana. "My father is going to flip out on me again."

"Rosana," said Steve. "This is the find of the century. Your father will be stunned when he hears what we've discovered. He won't have time to yell at you."

"You don't know that, Steve," said Rosana. "He can be a hard headed man."

"I'm coming with you, Rosana. Don't worry," assured Steve. "And if he does try to hit you, I'll deck him," said Steve with a smile trying to make Rosana feel more at ease.

Steve and the girls walked down to the village and went to Milena's parents' house. Milena's parents were surprised to see Steve as he rarely came into the village.

"Angelo, we have something very important to discuss with you and Rosana's parents," said Steve. "Can you please call them and ask them to meet us here at your house?"

Angelo and Mira were a bit worried as to why Steve wanted to talk to them, but Angelo obliged Steve and telephoned Rosana's parents. They trusted Steve and were thankful that he looked after the girls. The two families were old friends since Rosana and Milena spent so much time together. Both families treated the girls as their own, so they were concerned not only for Milena, but Rosana as well. Angelo asked Rosana's parents to join them as Steve had something very important to discuss with both families.

When Marko and Ana arrived, they had a concerned look on their faces. They saw Steve and the girls there and wondered what could have possibly happened to bring Steve down from the mountain again. They had many questions and no answers.

They all gathered in the kitchen and sat around the table. Mira made coffee for everyone and put out some of the pastries she baked. Steve introduced the subject of discussion very gently to the girls' parents. He wanted the parents to know, first and foremost, that the girls are in no danger.

"Angelo, Marko," he began. "The girls, myself and Butch went to the cave today. Now before you say anything… I want to tell you that what we found is guaranteed to blow your mind, and that it's all good."

"Okay, okay…What is it, man? Speak up!" exclaimed Marko impatiently. "This better be good because Rosana is in a world of trouble already."

"Marko!" snapped his wife, Ana. "Shut up and listen to what the man has to say."

"Marko, Angelo, we found a secret chamber filled with treasure," he said and paused to give the statement a chance to penetrate in their minds. "There is so much of it that we believe it's the Knights Templar lost treasure," Steve said, again pausing. This time noticing the bewildered look in both sets of parents' eyes. "We came to that conclusion because we found what resembled the Knights Templar cross, and just the sheer magnitude of the treasure, is truly incredible. However, we weren't the first ones to discover the treasure because we also found a pile of cocaine in the chamber."

The two couples just stared at Steve trying to comprehend what he just told them.

"Oh dear God," said Ana who was the first to find her voice. She looked at Rosana and came over to hug her.

"Are you alright my sweet child," she asked.

"Yes, Mom. I'm fine," said Rosana, thankful that her father didn't lose his cool.

"Here's what I think happened," said Milena. "I think that Mario, the dead man, somehow found the secret chamber. According to what the police told us, he was from the island of Ugljan and spent a lot of time here in Nevidane, and in that cave, as a kid. But didn't necessarily know about the chamber. I think that before he fled from Zadar, he somehow figured out the boulder was the doorway to a chamber and found a way to open it, like we did. Who knows? Maybe he even hid out in the cave for a period of time before he fled because he was a wanted man in Zadar. Once he got into the drug business, and they scored a big heist, he came back here and put the cocaine in there for safe keeping because he figured if the treasure was still there, then no one knew about the hidden chamber, and rightfully so. I don't know if he realized that the treasure was part of the lost treasure from the Knights Templar. Even if he didn't realize it, I'm sure he knew it was of great value. So, when the other three men came looking for the cocaine, he didn't want to divulge where it was because he didn't want them to see the treasure," continued Milena as she looked for signs of comprehension from her and Rosana's parents.

Steve then interjected, "With that much cocaine, I think they may have stolen it from the Italian drug cartel—they work closely with the Mexican cartels—and were planning to sell it in Europe on their own and keep the proceeds from the sale, but that's just a guess."

"But since Mario didn't want to tell them where it was hidden, they tortured him for the answer and in the process, they wound up strangling him with the wire around his neck," said

Rosana, picking up the story from where Milena and Steve left off.

"But how did the other men know about the cave?" Angelo asked.

"Maybe Mario told them he was going to hide the cocaine in the cave, thinking he would bury it somewhere in there. But maybe Mario didn't discover the secret chamber until after he had the cocaine and was searching for a place to stash it," reasoned Rosana.

"Either that, or Mario never actually told them he was going to stash anything in the cave. He may have fondly told them stories of how much he liked visiting the cave when he was a kid, but didn't say specifically that he would put the cocaine in the cave. So, the criminals came to the cave on the off chance that the coke might be there," countered Milena.

"Or," said Rosana, "He could have told them he'd meet them somewhere in Italy to divi up the cocaine amongst the four of them, but instead, he fled with all the cocaine and hid it in the cave thinking they would never figure it out. However, when the drug dealers went to meet Mario in Italy, Mario never showed up. Then they must have deducted that he skipped out with the drugs and took a chance on coming to the cave to see if the drugs were hidden there. And, maybe the reason we found Mario dead by the statue is because the other three dealers were hiding behind the rock walls just waiting to ambush Mario when he entered the cave. That's the only way they were ever going to find the cocaine… by torturing him. Only, hot-headed Alex went too far and wound-up strangling Mario to death."

Mira and Ana, who had remained silent during the news, looked on in wide eyed amazement at the scenarios that girls were telling.

"Umm," said Marko, his head spinning from trying to keep up. "You seem to have all the scenarios covered and they all sound feasible."

"There's got to be about 70 kilograms of cocaine there and that's worth about ten million U.S. dollars," said Steve. You know damn well that was stolen from the cartel. It takes a large operation to produce and move that much cocaine."

'*How does Steve know so much about cocaine?*' wondered Rosana.

"I think we should let the police handle this," said Marko. "I really don't want Rosana to have anything further to do with this."

"But, Dad, these cops are in over their heads. At the very least, they should have brought in a homicide detective from Zadar whose handled murder cases before. These cops have zero experience with stuff like this," said Rosana.

"Rosana, honey, I agree with your father," said Ana.

Milena parents also agreed with Marko, much to Rosana's and Milena's chagrin.

After much back-and-forth discussion, the decision was made to bring their story to the police, despite Rosana's protest.

"If we bring it to the police, I can almost guarantee you that they will steal some of the artifacts and the cocaine. I don't trust them one bit. For all we know, they may run off with all of it and leave the country without ever reporting it," said Rosana. She was upset with the decision to call in the police before they even had a chance to figure out a better way to handle it.

"There is too much there to carry off," said Steve. "They may take a few pieces—I wouldn't put it past them—but there's no way they could carry off that much treasure without someone seeing them. It would take weeks to discreetly move that massive amount of treasure. You know how nosey the people here are. You can't fart without the whole village knowing about it."

"I guess you're right," said Rosana, "but I'm not convinced that this is the best approach."

"If you have a better suggestion, speak up," said her father who was annoyed at his daughter for going against the majority vote.

"I think we should call an antiquities expert from the Archaeological Museum in Zagreb, and leave the cops out of it," said Rosana in defiance, "so they can give us a professional definitive answer as to whether it really is part of the lost treasure from the Knights Templar, and if so, what the treasure is worth. For all we know, it could all be costume jewelry."

"OH PLEASE!" yelled her father." Who would put costume jewelry into a hidden vault? Do you even hear yourself?" He clearly had no patience for his rebellious daughter. And because of Marko, Rosana's suggestion fell by the wayside.

Rosana had no choice but to go with the adult's opinion of calling the police. Though she was out voted, she knew in her heart of hearts that it was the wrong decision. She had no trust in the local police, and was convinced those two cops were corrupt.

"It's settled then," said Steve. "Now who's going to make the call?"

COPS AND ROBBERS

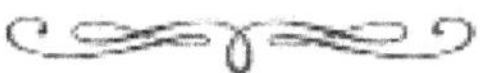

The following day, the police came back to the village. They met up with both Rosana's and Milena's parents, along with Steve and the girls, in the town center. But as in all small towns, when the police make a visit, everyone knows about it. And since the police had come to the village several times over the past week, the townspeople were beyond curious as to what was going on. Very quickly, a small group of villagers approached Officer Hrenek to ask questions.

"We hardly ever see the police and now you've already been here multiple times in the last few days," said Nino, the general store owner. "What is going on? Something is going on that you aren't telling us."

Viktor, the man who ran the fish cart, joined in. "We find it very curious that Rosana's and Milena's parents are going up the mountain with you this time. Are you going to tell us the truth or keep lying to us?" he asked.

Officer Hrenek was not pleased at having the villagers demand answers when he wasn't ready to divulge any information yet.

"When we have more information, you'll be the first to know," Hrenek said in a stern voice. "In the meantime, DO NOT follow us as you'll contaminate the crime screen."

"Nino, there is nothing to be concerned about," said Radic calmly. "We will let you know once we investigate the scene of the crime further."

The officers made it sound as if they found more evidence about the identity of the man, but of course, the police already knew who the dead man was, but the villagers didn't know that yet. The officers just didn't want to have to deal with a crowd of people coming up to the cave, and that's exactly what would happen if they knew it involved treasure.

As they ascended the mountain, Rosana couldn't help worrying about the decision they made to tell those local incompetent cops of what they found in the cave. *'I really think we should have called the Zagreb Museum and asked them to send an antiquities specialist to look at the treasure. I think it's the lost Knights Templar treasure, and if those crooked cops get their grubby hands on it, they will steal some of it, I just know it. I don't trust those cops for nothing,'* she thought.

Marko was still annoyed and worried that Rosana disobeyed him by going up to the cave after he told her not to. *'That girl is out of control,'* he thought. *'What am going to do? I leave soon to go back on the ship and won't be around to keep an eye on her. Ana doesn't seem to care that Rosana runs wild. That's the problem. That's why Danica drowned that day. Ana wasn't paying attention.'*

Ana wasn't concerned about what they would see in the cave. She trusted Rosana because she knew that Rosana made smart decisions. *'Heck, Rosana is the one who was quick to come up with an escape plan when those criminals took her and Milena hostage. Marko doesn't give her enough credit. Besides, she isn't a child anymore. She is almost an adult and I trust her,'* she thought.

Meanwhile, Angelo and Mira were quietly chatting on the way up.

"Do you really think they found the lost Knights Templar treasure?" Mira asked her husband while trying to contain her excitement. She was as much an adventurer as her daughter and this was the most exciting thing that ever happened in her lifetime. If this really was the Knights Templar treasure, it would be an event she would long remember. Though she still longed to visit far away places, this adventure of a lifetime was more than she ever thought she'd have. She couldn't contain her excitement at the prospect.

"I don't know, but I'm getting excited just thinking about it," said Angelo. "The only thing that worries me is the publicity that we will get if, in fact, it is the Knights Templar treasure. You know this is going to go viral on the internet and all sorts of weirdos will be showing up here, not the mention the hordes of media people that will swarm like insects onto the island. It's going to be a nightmare."

"Well, I'm not that worried about it because it will pass. Nothing lasts forever," said Ana. "But what does worry me is the cocaine they found. Whoever is missing the cocaine is sure to come looking for it. It's amazing that even our small island couldn't escape the drug epidemic. I always thought it was only the cities that had that problem. But now, it has found its way here. That's scary. And what's scarier is the goons that came looking for the cocaine. As if that wasn't bad enough, can you imagine what will happen when the drug lords send in their big guns? We need to make sure that Milena does NOT go near the cave. She needs to stay home until this whole thing blows over."

Steve, who was walking alone with Butch at his side, was deep in thought. *'This thing with the cocaine really has me worried. I've been in law enforcement long enough to know that the drug lords aren't going to sit still for a stunt like those criminals pulled off. They will send their enforcers to find the three men and to torture them until they divulge where they hid the cocaine. I also don't trust these cops. I agree with Rosana that they are incompetent,'* he said to himself.

Unbeknownst to the others, Steve had worked as an undercover narc, back in New York, before he was put on this island through the witness protection program for testifying against a crooked senator working with the drug cartels. That's why he knew so much about drugs.

"This better not be a joke of some kind," said Hrenek to Radic. "I don't enjoy climbing mountains."

"Oh, just relax. Exercise is good for you and you need it. Aren't you in the least bit curious as to what they found in the cave? If it really is the Knights Templar treasure, this will make world news and we will be famous," said Radic.

When they reached the cave and looked inside, they saw several men from the village already milling around the cave.

"What the hell are they doing here?" said Hrenek in frustration to Radic. "We told those idiots to keep away from the cave, and here they are anyway," he said throwing his hands up in the air. "Listen up people!" he said to the crowd in his most authoritative voice. "You all have to leave. This is a crime scene and we can't have you disturbing any evidence we may find."

"You sure are taking your sweet time figuring this out, Hrenek," yelled Ante, one of men from the village. "Maybe this case is over your head. You should call the senior investigators from Zadar. You know, we have children that sometimes come up here. I'd hate to see something happen to one of them because you are dragging your heels."

"Excuse me, Sir… you're Ante, aren't you?" asked Hrenek.

"Yes, I am," responded Ante in a defiant voice.

"If you keep talking like that, you're going to start a riot, and then I'll have to put you in jail!" said Hrenek. He spoke loud enough so the other men could hear. "Now, I suggest you and your friends leave here before I lock you all up."

After giving the cops dirty looks, the crowd of men descended the mountain and headed toward the village below. None of them could afford to be locked up when there was a harvest to bring in.

Once everyone was gone, Steve led everyone into the cave. He went directly to the boulder, as did the girls.

'Now before we show you the treasure, I'd like to show you how we came to the conclusion that it's the lost Knights Templar treasure," said Steve. "We dug over there," he said pointing to the spot where they had found the rock with the carvings. "We found a rock, which we covered up again, but the rock had carvings of a cross that resembled the Templar cross, and had a carving of a keystone."

He proceeded to tell them the story of the Templars, in case they weren't familiar with it, and then he took them over to the boulder. Hrenek, still skeptical of any treasure, listened with his arms crossed across his chest and one side of his mouth curled up as if doubtful that there was any treasure, or that what they found could possibly be the Knights Templar treasure.

"Then, up here, I found a carving of the cross again," said Steve excitedly as he pointed to the top of the boulder. "That's what convinced us that someone carved those things into the rock and into the boulder as clues as to where to find the treasure."

With that, Steve and the girls pulled on the boulder like before, and to the amazement of their parents and the police, it opened.

The girls and Steve stepped aside and let the police officers go past them, followed by the parents. When the police officers entered the chamber, they stopped dead in their tracks. Angelo walked around them and when he saw what the officers were looking at, he too stopped in his tracks taking it all in. With that the rest of the group filed in one by one. They too were awestruck at what they saw.

The parents' reaction was exactly what the girls expected. Awe and disbelief at what their eyes were seeing. There were loud gasps and 'Ohhh, dear God' exclamations from their parents and the officers. Radic, who had a camera around his neck, just stood there. He didn't react. Hrenek proceeded to walk over to one of the open trucks and started to examine its contents. Radic, still awestruck, slowly walked over to where Hrenek was standing.

"Do you think it's real?" he asked Hrenek.

"I don't know," replied Hrenek, "but you'd better start taking some pictures so we can document this."

"I didn't understand the magnitude of your discovery until now," admitted Marko to his daughter. Rosana found this to be a very humble and unexpected admission from her father because normally he thought he knew everything and never admitted any fault or misunderstanding.

After Ana and Mira saw the extent of what was in the secret chamber, they too were speechless.

"We have to contact the Archaeological Museum in Zagreb and have them come look at this treasure," said Radic as if in a trance. "And we will take the cocaine into custody at the station," he said earnestly after he got over the initial shock of seeing the magnitude of the chamber's contents.

"Well, I hate to break up this moment, but we all need to get back to our lives in the village until the authorities from Zagreb get here," said Officer Hrenek.

Rosana wasn't at all comfortable with the two officers. Hrenek in particular was being too hasty with this revelation. Why was Hrenek in such a rush to get back to the village when they just showed him the most important discovery of the century? In her eyes, they weren't trustworthy. And she wasn't wrong.

They all walked back down the mountain in silence, each of them lost in their own thoughts.

When they got to Steve's place, Hrenek turned to the group and said, "Now folks, let's remember that we need to keep this quiet until the antiquities expert comes to validate what is actually in the cave. We don't want people to get excited and go to the cave to look for the treasure."

They all agreed and Steve was the first to say his goodbyes. When the rest of them got back to the village, they said their farewells and went their separate ways. As the officers walked to their police car, a group of village men approached them.

"We demand to know what's going on," said Nino, the shop owner from earlier who appeared to be the group's spokesperson.

"Look everyone, as we told you before, as soon as we know anything, we will tell you. In the meantime, the cave is off limits for your own safety. There is a killer on the loose. I suggest you keep your doors and windows locked at night, and not let your kids go wandering up into the mountains," he said, hoping that would scare the villagers and that they would take him seriously. He didn't want anyone up there except himself and Radic.

The folks from the village were surprised at the answer they received from Hrenek. They had never had to worry about their safety before. Solemnly, they dispersed and returned to the shelter and safety of their homes.

As the officers were driving back to the police station, Officer Hrenek had a long talk with Officer Radic.

"Do you like working as a cop?" asked Hrenek as he gripped the steering wheel.

"Yes, I do, why?" replied Radic.

"I don't," said Hrenek. "I've worked this job for 25 years and find it unrewarding. People just bitch about their neighbors stealing their animals or some other nonsense. I'm tired of it. Furthermore, when I retire, I'll still have to watch my pennies. Retirement benefits are good, but not enough for a person to really enjoy their golden years in style."

"What are you getting at?" asked Radic.

"Look, we have the opportunity of a lifetime staring us in the face. Don't you want to get married someday and don't you want your family to be able to enjoy the finer things in life?" asked Hrenek.

"Of course, but what opportunity are you talking about?" asked Radic in his innocent confusion.

"The treasure, you idiot!" replied Hrenek. "Don't be so damn I. We can take some of the treasure and no one would even miss it since there's so much there," Hrenek said as his eyes began to glaze over as if he was crazed.

"You're insane," said Radic. "You want to steal historical treasure after a lifetime of devoting your life to law and order? And you think no one will notice? I guess you think everyone is stupid, huh? You'll never get away with it."

"You're so I. Grow up, will you?" replied Hrenek. "Do you really want to stay on this nothing island all your life and marry who… a peasant girl? You're a handsome guy and you can have any girl you want, especially if you had money. I think even that Milena girl has eyes for you. Come on, we don't have to stay on this island. We can get out of the country entirely and live anywhere we want and have whatever our hearts desire. You could even marry a supermodel and buy a yacht with the type of money you'll have. You can hob-nob with all the rich elite in Monaco, if you wanted to. HELL! You'd BE the rich elite!"

Radic went silent and gazed out the window. Reluctantly, he started to think about what Hrenek was proposing. Money, a supermodel, a yacht, living the high life drinking champagne and eating caviar, and living in any country he wanted; it sounded pretty damn good.

Radic turned to Hrenek. "You really think I could land a supermodel?" he asked.

"Probably more than one," Hrenek said as he winked and flashed a big smile.

So, they made a pact not to tell anyone about the treasure—not their police chief, not their family, nobody. And certainly, they weren't going to contact the museum in Zagreb. It was to remain a complete covert operation so they could leave the country without anyone suspecting anything or knowing where they were. Hrenek said that he would send for his family once they unloaded the merchandise.

"Good," said Hrenek. "Now give me the camera."

Radic gave the camera to Hrenek who proceed to take out the SD memory card and stuffed it in his shirt pocket.

"This disk will be burned when I get home. No one will ever have proof of how much treasure there was," he said with a sinister smile.

Later that day, the officers went up to the cave on their own, without telling anyone about it. They took the western road up the mountain to avoid anyone seeing them, with the intent to fill up a few satchels with some artifacts from the Knights Templar treasure.

As they approached the entrance of the cave, they saw beams of light in the rear of the main chamber from three different light sources. At first, they thought it may be some of the men from the village, but in listening to them speak, Hrenek realized it wasn't anyone from the village because they were conversing in German.

"They are speaking in German!" whispered Hrenek, surprised to hear a foreign language. "I bet they're the criminals that the girls told us about."

Radic and Hrenek crept into the cave slowly and quietly so as not to alert the three men who were holding the flashlights. Their intent was to surprise the criminals and over power them. They were agitated that these criminals were spoiling their plans.

Suddenly, Pete felt the hairs on the back of his neck stand up. He sensed he and his buddies were no longer alone. Unsure of why he felt this way, he turned his flashlight toward the entrance of the cave and caught a glimpse of a shadow.

"Who's there?" cried out Pete while pointing his gun at the direction of the officers. When Alex and Joe heard Pete, they jumped, turned toward the front of the cave, and fumbled for their guns which were tucked into the back of their pants. They raised their guns just in time to hear Hrenek giving Pete orders to drop his gun.

"Pasman police! Drop your gun and put your hands over your head," yelled Hrenek in his bad cop voice as he stepped out of the shadows to confront the criminals. "And that goes for the rest of you too."

Determined not to get caught by the police, Alex released the safety from his gun and pressed on the trigger. His bullet whizzed through the air, barely missing Hrenek.

"Holy shit!" thought Hrenek, who felt how close the bullet came to him.

The officers already had their guns ready in one hand and held their flashlights with the other. They shot a few shots toward the men and then turned and ran out of the cave. Once outside the cave, they crouched and hid behind some bramble bushes, their guns still in the ready position so they could fire at will when the men decided to come out of the cave.

"Now we have an advantage over the criminals because we can see them come out of the cave, but the criminals can't see us,' thought Hrenek.

'They're shooting at us!' realized Radic, much to his surprise. This was a sleepy, peaceful island with no crime. This was the first time he'd ever been shot at and he was determined not to be killed. *'You trained for this. Now snap out of it. You know what to do,'* he said to himself mustering up the courage to be cop-like.

Meanwhile, inside the cave, the three criminals were planning their next move.

"What are the cops doing here?!" Pete exclaimed.

"I don't know, but we have to rush them and flood them with bullets," said Alex. "There's no way I'm giving everything up now."

Joe and Pete nodded nervously.

"Okay, on three we go and we go fast," Alex said. "We don't know where the cops are hiding, so I'll shoot straight. Pete, you shoot left. And Joe, you shoot right. We need to take them out and then get what's ours. Ready? One … two … three!"

With that the three men ran toward the cave entrance. With each step their adrenaline rose, making them feel invincible. As soon as they reached the opening to the outside world, the bright sunlight blinded them, but it didn't stop them. They pressed the triggers of their guns, with each firing in a different direction.

But the officers were ready and waiting for them. And though there were only two of them compared to the gang's three men, the officers, who had the advantage of being hidden, returned fire immediately.

Unable to see where the officers were crouched, the three men scurried to find protection from the gunshots that rang out toward them.

"Oh shit," yelled Pete as he saw Hrenek rise from his hiding spot and pointing his gun right at him. Pete ducked and was just about to turn his direction when Hrenek pulled the trigger. In less than a second, the bullet zipped through the air and pierced Pete's forehead. Pete's eyes and mouth opened wide as his arms flung in the air, and then his entire body fell to the ground with a loud thud, limp and lifeless in an instant.

"One down. Two to go," Hrenek said with a crazed smile.

Hrenek then turned his sights onto Joe, who was trying to hide behind a tree. Joe's back was to the tree, and if he had moved half a step more to the right, Hrenek might not have been able to spot him. But since the left side of Joe's body was visible from behind the tree, Hrenek focused on his upper left back area, hoping he'd hit his heart. Like a skilled marksman, Hrenek aimed, took a breath, slightly opened his mouth without exhaling, and then pulled the trigger. Within a second Joe fell to the ground, holding his left shoulder and screaming in pain.

But while Hrenek was so focused on Joe, he didn't realize that Alex was focused on him. Alex had just witnessed his friend Pete get killed and now his friend Joe get seriously injured. Alex was determined to take out this cop. Alex stepped out from behind the boulder he was crouched behind and aimed his gun squarely at Hrenek's back. Radic saw Alex appear from behind the boulder and what he was about to do.

"Hrenek! Behind you!" Radic yelled.

Hrenek turned and raised his gun. But before he could shoot it, he felt a piecing pain just below his right shoulder. Alex had good aim too.

Upon seeing what just happened, Radic raised his gun and aimed for Alex. His aim was not as sharp as Hrenek's, but he fired and hit Alex in the left thigh.

As Alex fell to the ground, he dropped his gun and gripped both hands around his badly bleeding leg.

Radic sprinted over to Hrenek. "Let me see your wound. Is it bad?" Radic frantically asked.

"God damn it I'm fine. Go tie those bastards up."

But Hrenek wasn't fine. The blood was pulsing out of his arm fast. Fearing that Hrenek might bleed out, Radic ripped off Hrenek's sleeve from his wounded arm and tied it tightly around Hrenek's shoulder, as a tourniquet to stop the bleeding. Then he set his sights on the two injured criminals.

Like a gazelle, he sprinted over to Joe, who was now crawling on the ground trying to find cover and hide. Radic grabbed him by his leg and said, "Not so fast." He pulled Joe toward him. Joe screamed out in pain as his belly was dragged on the ground, forcing his arms up over his head.

"My shoulder!" he yelled. "You assholes shot me!"

"I'm gonna do worse than that if you don't shut up and cooperate," Radic yelled. He wasn't used to being so gruff with people, but a part of him liked it.

Radic straddled Joe's lower back, pulled his uninjured arm down first to cuff it, and then a little more gently brought down the injured arm to lock the cuffs in place.

"Stay here," he said, leaving Joe handcuffed and face down in the dirt.

Radic then ran over to Alex who was now searching for the gun he had dropped.

"Where is it? Where is it? Come on … where is it?" Alex mumbled frantically as he searched for his fallen gun.

With his eagle eye vision, Radic spotted the gun in a small grassy patch. He leaped over Alex on the ground and with one fell swoop, reached down with his left arm and picked up the gun.

"I guess you're looking for this?" Radic said teasingly to Alex as he held up the gun.

"I swear I'll kill you," Alex snarled.

"Maybe … but not today," said Radic as he grabbed Alex's hands and used a zip-tie to secure them behind his back.

Alex flinched in pain.

"Don't be a baby," Radic said with a slight chuckle. "It's your leg that I shot, not your arm."

Radic took a moment to catch his breath. He couldn't believe what he had just done. In his entire career he had handcuffed a few drunks who were determined to drive. But he had never shot anyone nor handcuffed actual criminals. His whole body felt like it was pulsing with electricity.

With both criminals restrained, Radic tended to their wounds. He ripped the bottom half of Alex's shirt off and then tore it further into strips. He used the strips to make tourniquets to stop their bleeding. He then took out the first aid kit he always carried in his backpack and bandaged the wounds on Alex's leg and on Joe's shoulder. Radic then dragged them one-by-one into the cave. The entire time Alex screamed obscenities at Radic while Joe pleaded to be let go. Radic simply ignored them. He pulled out the rope from his backpack and tied the men to the friar statue with their backs facing the friar. He tied the rope around their waists and their chests to be sure they couldn't get free.

Radic then went outside to speak with Hrenek, who was sitting next to a boulder nursing his wound. The officers spoke in Croatian so that the criminals couldn't understand them.

"Good job, Radic," Hrenek said. "I think this kind of excitement suits you."

"I don't know about that," said Radic. "How are we going to get the stuff out of the chamber with these two guys here?"

"Oh, for Christ's sake," said Hrenek, "just when I thought you finally grew a pair. Just blindfold them so they can't see where we are going."

"Good idea," said Radic. He felt foolish for even asking the question, but he wasn't used to this type of stuff and, by now, he was more stressed than excited. After all, he had never been in a gun fight before, but apparently, Hrenek was.

Radic went back into the cave and knelt by Joe.

"Hey man," Joe said pleadingly. "Can't you just let me go. I'll just disappear and you'll never hear from me again. I promise."

"Shut your mouth!" Alex yelled at Joe.

Radic ignored them both and quickly ripped some of Joe's clothing off and made blindfolds and gags from the material. He wrapped the makeshift blindfold over each man's eyes and gagged them both.

"Radic!" Hrenek's voice yelled in Croatian. "Let's do this!"

Radic saw Hrenek slowly walking into the cave. "Are you okay to walk?" he asked.

"Of course! My legs aren't shot. I'm just a little woozy, but I can still do this. Go get the bags from outside."

Radic did as he was told and then the two officers walked to the large boulder inside the cave.

"Do you remember what Steve did to open this thing?" asked Hrenek.

"I think so," said Radic as he pushed and pulled on the boulder. But the boulder wouldn't budge. "Damn. Steve made it look easy."

"Here, let me try too."

The two men struggled with the boulder for a few minutes. Feeling frustrated after all they had just done and not wanting to lose at this point, Radic threw his whole body against the boulder at just the right angle and it effortlessly swung open.

"See?" said Radic. "I told you I could do it."

The officers walked into the chamber, still feeling that sense of awe as before.

"Are you totally sure we should do this?" asked Radic, feeling a moment of doubt.

Hrenek turned to him. "We've been through this already. We're doing this. Take a bag and fill it."

Radic took one of the empty bags and started filling it with the ancient gold Aureus coins. He thought they would have the most value. Hrenek thought the ornate and jewel encrusted items such as necklaces, broches, crowns, and gold goblets would bring in a handsome amount of money.

"This stuff is heavy," noted Radic. "I hope we can carry it all."

"Stop complaining and take these bags to the car. Then come back and escort the criminals into the car. Then get me last," Hrenek ordered.

Officer Radic walked down to the car with one loaded bag in each hand. *"It's a good thing I work out,"* he thought. Even though he was relatively fit, the bags were heavy and Radic was already tired from the excitement of the day. He felt his muscles throbbing from exertion. The trek to the car and then back to the cave felt like a marathon to him. But he wasn't even close to done. He now had to walk both criminals down to the car. Since Alex couldn't walk on his injured leg, and he was handcuffed, Radic decided to carry him over his shoulder, using a fireman lift. Alex tried to scream through his gag the entire time. Radic didn't know if he was screaming in pain or just trying to be a jerk. He figured the latter.

"No one is out here to hear you," Radic told Alex. But Alex continued fighting and making noises the entire time. Radic put Alex in the back seat of the car and then went back up the mountain to get Joe.

Since Joe was shot in the arm, he was able to walk on his own. Radic led Joe slowly down to the car.

"I still have my gun," said Radic. "If you try to run, I'll shoot you."

Joe felt defeated at this point. He knew he shouldn't have gotten involved with Alex, but the allure of the money was too much to resist. Joe walked quietly to the car, his head down and his eyes soft. Radic felt a little sympathy for him. Upon getting to the car, Radic tied Joe's feet together as an extra precaution to keep him from trying to escape.

With both criminals locked in the back seat of the police car, Radic went up the mountain one last time to get his partner. As fit as he was, by now he was huffing and puffing with every step.

Hrenek was right where he had left him—in the chamber sitting against a rock. Hrenek appeared weak from the loss of blood and was now slumped over.

"Come on … let me help you up," he said to Hrenek. "Can you walk?"

"Yeah," was all Hrenek said, which actually concerned Radic a little.

"He must be really weak," Radic thought.

He stood beside Hrenek and grasped him around his waist. He positioned Hrenek's uninjured arm around his neck and assisted his long-time partner out of the cave and slowly down the mountain.

As they walked, they talked about what their next steps would be.

Once at the car, Radic enacted the plan. He immediately drove to the only urgent care center on the island.

As Radic pulled up to the clinic, he looked around. It was empty, with no other townspeople mulling around. Radic felt a sense of relief. *"Finally, something is going our way,"* he thought. The fewer people who saw them, the better.

Just then, the medic's dog came from around the building and barked at the car.

'Oh crap!' thought Radic. *'Shut up, you damn dog.'*

The medic on this island lived on the premises, so it wasn't unusual for the dog to be there or to bark, but Radic didn't like the attention the barking could attract.

Upon hearing the dog bark, the medic came out and waved. Radic opened his door, exited the vehicle, and greeted the medic. The two men carefully got Hrenek and the prisoners out of the car.

"What happened?" asked the medic, Sime, speaking in Croatian once they got the men inside the urgent care center.

Radic proceeded to tell Sime the story he and Hrenek had agreed upon during their walk to the car.

"We were on the west side of the mountain to investigate reports of strange men wandering the countryside and harassing people. We saw the men traveling up the mountain toward the cave and followed them. We recognized them as the criminals that Rosana and Milena described to us. That's when the three men started shooting at us."

"Three men?" asked Sime. "Where's the third man?"

"He's dead," said Radic. "I've called the coroner's office and they will be picking him up."

The medic treated Joe's wound first. "That's a pretty nasty wound," said the medic. "One more centimeter over and you would have been dead with a bullet in your heart." Joe was still gagged so he couldn't reply.

The medic examined Alex, who was also still gagged, as per the officers' request.

"They both need to be transported to Zadar," the medic said, "They're stable now but they'll both likely need surgery to remove the bullets, and we don't do that here."

Sime then looked at Hrenek's wound. "I think I can stitch you up and you'll be okay. The bullet mostly grazed you."

"Grazed him?" questioned Radic. "But he seemed so weak and like he was losing a lot of blood."

"He was probably more in shock than anything else. You know how even a little bit of blood can look like a lot when it runs onto clothing or when you're in a crisis situation, which it sounds like you were. He's really not that injured."

"Hmpf," was all Radic said.

After Hrenek's wound was treated, both officers went back to the police car. Hrenek had a newfound burst of energy and immediately grabbed the radio and called Steve.

"Steve, we got the bastards," he said gleefully boasting. He then proceeded to tell Steve the same story they told the medic. "You should have seen it, Steve," Hrenek continued. "Those bastards thought they could overpower us, but I shot two of them. I shot one guy right in the head and killed him and shot the other in the chest. Just barely missed his heart, the medic said. Thank goodness I was there." He then glanced at Radic and saw him glaring at him, "Of course, Radic got a few good shots in too," he added.

Hrenek and Radic drove to Angelo's house to give the family the same update. They told the same story to Marko and his family. Both families were relieved that the criminals were either dead or in the hospital. However, Rosana was more convinced than ever that the cops were lying.

As soon as the officers left, Rosana telephoned Milena and expressed her concern. "I know in my heart that the two cops didn't go up there to investigate reports of strange men harassing the residents," said Rosana. "The reason they were up there was to steal some of the treasure."

"Yes, I agree. I figured that they wanted to carry off as much of the treasure as they could before they reported it to anyone, including the museum," replied Milena.

"But at least now we know the criminals won't come after us any time soon," said Rosana. "One is dead and the other two are wounded and in the hospital in Zadar. And surely, they'll be taken to the police station jail after they're discharged from the hospital."

"Yes, that's true," said Milena.

"Hey, can you meet me at the Stari Zidi restaurant in an hour?" Rosana asked. "There's more I want to say without potential eavesdroppers here."

"Sure, I'll see you soon."

Meanwhile, back at the village, the news spread about the three criminals thanks to the medic's receptionist. She didn't know enough to keep her mouth shut and didn't know she was supposed to. She figured she would only tell one or two people, so what harm could that do. But as with all small towns, the telephone game ran rampant, as did the wild stories and exaggerations that went with it. Within a few mere hours, the village was abuzz with the news, with many wildly speculating about who those men were and why a gun fight took place.

Nino called the police station. "I need to speak with Office Hrenek right now," he demanded to the officer who answered. When he learned that neither Hrenek nor Radic were at the station, he demanded to know more about the gunfight that took place at the mountain.

"Gunfight?" the desk officer repeated. "We don't have any reports about a gunfight."

"Well can you look into it?" Nino questioned, "And then let me know what you find out?"

"We'll investigate and release any details we can." The officer replied.

Unsatisfied with what he found out, Nino went to the local café by the water where the men hung out and played cards. He sat down with a few of the men and listened to their conversation. They were abuzz with the story about the gunfight. Nothing like this had ever happened on this island so it was big news.

"They think we are stupid and don't know what's going on," said an older man with gray hair and a walrus mustache. His cigarette hung out of the corner of his mouth while he talked and played cards. "But I know it had to involve that bank robbery in Amsterdam. I'm not as stupid as that cop thinks I am."

"Yes," said his friend, who could have been his twin, "They think we are all country bumpkins. I heard on the news, just like everyone else, that there was a major bank heist in Amsterdam. I'm betting those men fled from Amsterdam and came here because they thought no one would look for them on this little island," said his card playing buddy.

"But I wonder why the first guy, the one they found dead in the cave, was murdered. Do you suppose that he betrayed the other three guys by taking all the money for himself and leaving them out in the cold?" asked the older man.

"Yes, I'll bet on it," replied his buddy. "When it comes to money, people get very greedy. It blinds them, and now he is dead because of it."

"Ain't that the truth," chimed in Nino. The three men laughed and nodded.

While the town's people knew about the bank robbery that took place in Amsterdam because they saw the newscast on the TV, they didn't know about the cocaine or the treasure, and Hrenek intended to keep it that way for as long as possible.

Just as planned, Rosana and Milena met at the Stari Zidi restaurant and ordered some food.

"How are we going to prove that the crooked cops took some of the artifacts?" asked Rosana as she nibbled on the olive hors d'oeuvres and bread in front of her.

"I don't know," replied Milena. "I guess no one will ever know unless they try to sell it. Don't worry about it though. God works in mysterious ways. They will get theirs in the end. I strongly believe that."

"That much wealth right there for the taking was too much for the cops to bear. It was almost as easy as taking candy from a baby," said Rosana.

"Or taking the prosciutto from your plate," Milena playfully said as she helped herself to Rosana's food.

— — —

Back at Steve's compound, Steve had a feeling that Rosana's fears were spot on. He found the whole hostage situation bothersome and was determined to do all he could to keep the girls safe from the criminals … and the cops. The fact that there was a gunfight between the officers and the criminals solidified his belief in what Rosana predicted. Therefore, the next day, bright and early, he went up to the cave with Butch and his rifle and hid behind one of the nearby chest-high rock walls. From his vantage point, he had a clear view to the cave entrance and to the path that led up the west side of the mountain.

"Well, Butch," he said to his dog, "now we wait."

Butch barked as if in agreement.

"But quietly, my friend. Quietly."

Butch cocked his head and wagged his tail. Steve couldn't help but to giggle at his loyal, strong, yet sometimes silly dog.

"I can always count on you to make me smile, Butch." He said as he patted Butch's head.

After an hour and a half of silence, Butch stood up and pointed his nose toward the cave.

"Shhh. Silence," Steve said to Butch in a whispered voice.

Steve carefully peaked out from behind the rock wall. What he saw didn't surprise him. Officers Hrenek and Radic emerged from the cave carrying overstuffed satchels. Steve knew those bags were filled with the lost treasure of the Templar's. Hrenek only carried satchels in his left hand because of the wound he received on his right shoulder. Radic was carrying heavy satchels in both hands.

"How many more loads are we going to take?" Radic asked.

"As many as I say we're taking," replied Hrenek. "There's so much in there no one is going to miss this."

Steve, determined to stop the crooked cops from stealing the treasure, carefully positioned his gun from behind the rock wall and aimed it at Radic's feet. He fired a warning shot.

"What the hell?' Radic screamed as he jumped and dropped his satchels.

Upon hearing the gunshot, Butch barked loudly and charged at Radic, grabbing onto Radic's leg.

"Arrrrgh!" cried Radic. "Where did this dog come from? … Butch? … Stop … Release … No …" He tried every command he could think to get the dog to let go, but Butch would only listen to Steve. The dog dug his teeth deeper and deeper into Radic's leg. Radic fell to the ground, which gave Butch an even better grip on his leg. The dog violently shook his head back and forth, like a wolf killing its prey. With each shake Radic screamed out in pain. He could feel his skin ripping and being shredded from the dog's razor-sharp teeth. Butch's grip was like a vice. There was nothing Radic could do. The more he struggled, the harder the dog latched on. Radic tried to keep still to stop the dog from biting harder.

With Butch keeping Radic busy, Steve focused on Hrenek.

"Drop the gun, Hrenek, and put your hands up," shouted Steve in his most commanding voice, "or I will shoot for your head."

"Okay, okay," Hrenek yelled back cautiously. "Don't shoot. We can work this out." Hrenek dropped the satchel and started squatting, as if he were going to obey the command. But instead, he reached for the gun in his holster and fired toward the rock wall. Since his right arm was injured, he had to use his non-dominant hand to fire, which made his aim not as sharp.

"You're very foolish, Hrenek," shouted Steve from behind the rock wall. "It doesn't have to be this way. Put the treasure back and no one has to know about this."

"Go to Hell, hermit," Hrenek yelled back and fired his gun at Steve again.

Steve, on the other hand, had the advantage of being behind the rock wall. He saw Hrenek's injured arm and aimed for that. He didn't want to kill anyone, and he thought hitting an already injured area would cause enough pain to make him surrender. Steve was a skilled hunter and marksman, so he pointed his gun toward Hrenek's upper right chest and pulled the trigger.

"Arrrrgh!" cried Hrenek. The bullet hit exactly where Steve intended. Hrenek's face contorted as the pain on the entire right side of his upper body was too much for him to bear. He dropped his gun and rolled onto his back grabbing his chest.

Steve took advantage of the moment. With Hrenek distracted by the pain, Steve ran toward Radic.

"Butch, release!" he commanded.

Butch immediately let go of Radic's leg just as Steve reached them. He bent down and grabbed Radic's arm and twisted it behind the officer's back. Steven quickly unhooked the handcuffs from Radic's belt. He cuffed the officer with his own handcuffs.

"Hey …. You can't do that!" Radic shouted at Steve. "I'm a police officer. Let me go right now or I'll arrest you."

"You're not a police officer," Steve snarled back. "You're a criminal. You should be ashamed of yourself. You don't deserve to wear that uniform."

As Hrenek laid on the ground in pain, he noticed that Steve was distracted with Radic. He knew now was his only opportunity to get them out of this predicament. He groped around for his gun, found it, and grabbed the gun. He then pointed it at Steve.

Butch sensed that Steve was in danger. He saw Hrenek pointing his gun at Steve and sprang into action to defend his master. Butch's gaze locked onto Hrenek and he raced toward the fallen officer. When he was a mere two feet away, he pushed off with his two hind legs and pounced in the air, set to land right on Hrenek.

Hrenek saw the dog mid-air, mouth open, pointed teeth ready to attack his jugular vein. Hrenek panicked, pointed his gun at the dog, and shot off two bullets into the leaping dog's belly. Butch yelped loudly and dropped to the ground right across Hrenek's lap.

Steve heard the bullets and turned, only to see his best friend landing lifeless on the officer.

"No!!!!" Steve yelled as he threw Radic to the ground. He locked his eyes on Hrenek. "You bastard! I will kill you with my bare hands!" Tears welled up in Steve's eyes as he ran toward Hrenek.

Hrenek saw the piercing crazed look on Steve's face and knew he was in trouble. Steve's brows were furrowed, his eyes squinted, and his lips snarled and upturned like a wild animal about to make his kill. Instinctively, Hrenek aimed his gun at Steve and fired off three shots at Steve's chest.

In Steve's rage, he didn't even feel the fatal bullet tear through his heart. All he knew was that he couldn't move anymore. He stopped mid-run, his arms flung backwards, his mind uncertain what was going on. His body waved like a sheet of paper in the wind, and then he dropped down just as the world around him went black.

Hrenek sat silent for a moment breathing heavily and taking in what had just occurred. He saw Radic about 20 feet away, handcuffed and bleeding badly from the ripped flesh of his dog bitten leg. He looked down at his own chest and saw the blood oozing out of him. He saw the dead dog at his feet and Steve's dead body a few feet away. He inhaled deeply to calm his nerves. This certainly wasn't what he had envisioned would happen today.

He used his left arm to push himself off the ground and then slowly walked over to Radic. He uncuffed Radic and looked at his leg.

"That brute thought he and his dog could take us on, HA!" said Hrenek with satisfaction in his voice.

"Man! That was Steve! You shot Steve! The entire island loves Steve! What the hell did you do?" said Radic.

"Shut up!" Hrenek yelled. "He was going to kill us. He got what he deserved."

"But what are we going to tell everyone?" Radic asked.

"Nothing. We'll be long gone by the time they find the bodies."

"Shit. We're not going anywhere like this," Radic said as he examined his wounds. "We need to stop the bleeding. That dog ripped up my leg. I'm in so much pain. I feel like I'm going to be sick."

They sat outside the cave and tended to their wounds as best as they could. Blood covered their clothes, the ground, their hands, their faces. It was like a sea of red in the middle of the lush green mountainside.

They rested in silence for several minutes, each thinking what to do next. Eventually Hrenek stood up and said, "Let's get these bodies inside the cave. I'm down an arm and you're down a leg. Between the two of us we make one healthy person, so we can do this."

Together, they struggled to drag Butch's and Steve's bodies into the cave. Then they gathered their satchels and made their way slowly down the west side of the mountain. Radic, who was usually fit and active, panted from the weariness and moaned in pain as he hobbled on his one good leg. Both men dragged their satchels behind them because they were too weak to carry them. After what seemed like an eternity, they reached the car. The two cops collapsed into the seats, breathing heavily. Their struggle to descend the mountain reopened their wounds and now blood and sweat covered their bodies. Radic pulled out the first aid kit from the car's glove compartment and tried to clean the reopened wounds on his leg with the tiny alcohol swabs. He helped Hrenek clean up his reopened chest wound too. He didn't see an exit hole on Hrenek's back and thought the bullet must still be inside Hrenek's chest.

"This is bad, Hrenek. This is really bad. How are we going to get out of this?" Radic asked.

"We'll stick with the plan," said Hrenek. "We'll mend our wounds as best as we can, then we'll change into the clean clothes we brought with us. This way no one will see our wounds or the blood. We will drive the car over to Tkon and drive onto the car ferry without getting out of the car. No one will be suspicious that way. Once we are in Biograd, we can go to an urgent care center there and get patched up better. From Biograd, we will drive down to Split. From there, we'll board a plane for Spain, like we planned."

"But won't the medic there ask us about our wounds?" asked Radic. "I think the bullet may still be inside you. I don't see an exit hole."

"Don't worry about that. If the medic asks, we'll tell him our prisoner escaped. Our story is that we were transporting a prisoner to the airport in Split and he grabbed one of our guns. Then he used the gun against us. I'm sure the medic in Biograd has heard about our gunfight with the criminals, so this will all make sense to him," said Hrenek. "Just stick to the plan. If the bullet is still inside me, I'll get it taken out in Spain."

"But what about my leg? Are we going to say the prisoner bit me? How do we explain this?" Radic asked pointing to his mangled leg that looked more like ground beef than skin at this point.

"Keep your leg covered. We'll get that taken care of in Spain too. The important thing right now is to just stick to the plan. Got it? Just stick to the plan."

- 6 -

GIRLS MEET DRUG LORD

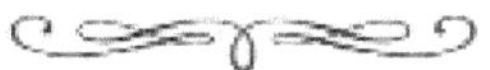

Three days later, the girls felt that something just wasn't right. They didn't know what, but the clues were there. The museum's antiquities curator hadn't arrived yet, and there were no newspaper or TV reporters on the island. They expected news crews from around the world to flock to the island in droves once the story broke about the discovery of the Knights Templar's lost treasure. But instead … nothing. It was boring business as usual on the island.

So, they decided to pay Steve a visit to find out if he had heard anything over his ham radio. Upon reaching the compound, the dogs barked as usual, but Butch was not with the pack.

"Where's Butch?" Rosana said.

Milena looked around, shook her head, and shrugged her shoulders.

"Butch! Butch! Come here boy!" Rosana shouted over the barking dogs.

Rosana gave the dogs their usual biscuit offerings to quiet them down. They hungerly devoured the biscuits, but the dogs wouldn't settle down. It was as if they were trying to tell the girls something.

"Where's Steve?" asked Rosana. "He's usually out by now when the dogs bark."

"I don't know. This seems strange," said Milena.

They walked up to Steve's house and knocked on the door. Silence.

"Something is wrong," said Rosana. "I can feel it."

"Maybe Steve and Butch went up on the mountain," replied Milena.

"Yeah, but the rest of the dogs never act like this. They sound meaner than usual. I'm a little worried," said Rosana.

"Maybe he went back to the cave to check on the treasure."

"There's only one way to find out."

They quickly made their way further up the mountain, but didn't see Steve or Butch anywhere. As they approached the cave, they both stopped dead in their tracks.

"Look at all this blood," said Milena as she surveyed the area and saw small pools of coagulated blood on the grass. "What do you suppose happened here?"

"I don't know, but I don't like it. Look at the way the vegetation is all flattened out around where the blood is. Looks like someone was dragged into the cave while they were bleeding," said Rosana. "We should leave. I have a bad feeling about this."

"We came all this way to find Steve," said Milena. "Maybe he's in trouble and needs help. We can't just turn around and go home without checking it out."

"Okay," said Rosana, "but I really don't want to go in there."

They took their flashlights out of their jacket pockets and hung them on their belt loop. Carefully and slowly, they walked into the cave.

Rosana was the first to scream.

"What's wrong?" Milena franticly asked. She then turned her head to where Rosana was looking and gasped.

Right there, several yards inside the entrance of the cave, were Steve and Butch, both laying in a pool of blood. Steve was on his back, his face turned to the side and his arms still above his head from when he was dragged in. Butch was at his feet, laying on his side.

"Steve!" Milena yelled as she ran to his body. Rosana was right behind her.

The girls knelt next to him, one on each side, his blood all over their pants and legs now. Instinctively, Milena started doing chest compressions on him. "One, two, three, four, five, six …" she counted out loud with each compression. When she hit 30, she put her lips upon his lifeless mouth and blew in two breaths. "Come on, Steve. You'll be okay," she said through tears.

Milena put her hands back on his chest to do more compressions. Rosana gently put her hand on top of Milena's and said softly, "I don't think that's going to do anything, Milena."

Milena looked up and locked eyes with Rosana. Reluctantly, she nodded slowly. Her focused and furrowed brow softened and despair set in. She sat back on her folded legs. Her arms went limp and her hands rested on her lap as she lowered her head and sobbed.

Rosana put her hands over her face and cried out with big hard sobs of pain and despair. Her entire body shook as the tears ran down her face and onto her hands.

Milena made the sign of the cross with her right hand's fingertips; she touched her forehead, middle chest, left shoulder, right shoulder and then her middle chest again. Rosana brought her hands from her face and did the same. She then reached down and put her left hand on Steve's arm and tearfully said, "Rest in peace, my friend." She leaned slightly to her right, toward Steve's feet, and petted Butch's fur with her right hand and said, "You, too, Butch."

Due to the dimness of the cave entrance and their shock and tears, they didn't even see the man sitting on the floor with his back against the wall, just a few yards from them.

"I didn't do this," the man said softly, while looking down at the gun he was holding in his lap.

The girls froze. They recognized the voice and the accent. They quickly jumped up, wiped the tears from their faces, and turned toward the voice. Milena shone her flashlight toward the far cave wall and scanned until she saw the man in the light. It was Joe.

"What are you doing here?" asked Milena as confusion took over her fear. "We thought you were in the hospital."

"I was," said Joe. "But that hospital is a joke. I was able to walk out in the middle of the night. No one was guarding my door … such a joke!" He gave a slight chuckle as he shook his head. He paused and motioned to Steve and Butch. "I don't know what happened to that man and his dog," he said in a low soft voice. "I was ordered to come back here to find the cocaine. They told me that if I came back empty handed, they would kill me." Tears were beginning to well in his eyes. "But when I got here, I found those two … dead. I don't know who killed them."

"Who is 'they'?" asked Milena.

"The Italian-drug lord," Joe replied halfheartedly. "I looked everywhere and there's no coke here. I think Mario hid the coke someplace else with the intention of keeping it for himself so he could sell it here in Croatia, but now he's dead and there's no way for me to find out where it is."

"So, you're from Italy. I thought so ... from your accent," Milena added quickly.

"Well, it's not here," Rosana blurted out matter-of-factly. "We thought money was hidden here. We had no idea it was cocaine. But, in any event, you're right. There's nothing here. We searched as well."

"I can't go back empty handed," Joe said. "They will kill me as sure as the sun will come up tomorrow." He slumped against the wall, defeated and downhearted. "I don't know what I'm going to do. I might as well get it over with and put a bullet in my head," he said looking down again at the gun he was holding in his lap.

"No, no, don't do that!" said Rosana as she held out her hand and shook her hand and her head simultaneously as if to stop him. "Can't you flee to another country where they won't be looking for you? Maybe go to Australia or America."

"And how would I get there?" he asked sarcastically, making hand gestures while waving his gun in the air. His finger was on the trigger and that caught Rosana's eye. She felt her stomach drop and her heart beat faster.

"I haven't got that kind of money," he said. "Plus, thanks to you and your friend, my face is plastered all over the wanted posters for robbery, but I never robbed a bank. It's almost comical."

"You must have family and friends. Why don't you borrow some money from them?" asked Rosana as she slowly and casually moved closer to Joe in an attempt to grab his gun out of his waving hand.

"Look," said Milena who clearly had enough of this chit-chat. Now she was livid. "I couldn't give a rat's ass about your problems. Our friend is laying here DEAD. Do you hear me? DEAD!" she yelled. "And all because of you and your low-life cohorts! You want to kill yourself? Be my guest, you piece of shit! You come to my island with your cocaine and bring death and destruction to our friends and you expect us to feel sorry for you. DROP DEAD!"

"MILENA!" shouted Rosana as she switched to Croatian so Joe couldn't understand what she was about to say. "Are you crazy? He has a gun in his hand. I was trying to win his confidence and maybe take his gun away from him. The man is in serious trouble, and if he feels like he can trust us, we can use that to our advantage and overpower him in his moment of weakness," said Rosana.

"You're the one that's crazy, Rosana. What if we can't overpower him? Do you think he'll think twice before shooting us? We need to get outta here before this gets any crazier."

Rosana returned her attention to Joe and said in English, "Look, my friend is really upset over the death of our friend. I think it's best if I take her home. You should get out of here and find someplace else to hide. Once news of Steve's death gets out, this place is gonna be crawling with cops. As far as we're concerned, we never saw you today. Good luck to you."

She grabbed Milena's arm and quickly led her out of the cave. With each step she glanced over her shoulder and looked in the direction of Joe's flashlight to make sure he wasn't pointing his gun at them.

Once outside the cave, the girls ran as fast as they could to a boulder several yards away and knelt behind it to hide. They wanted some protection in case Joe decided to come outside looking for them.

"Do you believe him?" asked Milena. "Do you think he's telling the truth or do you think he shot them?"

"I don't know who or what to believe at this point," replied Rosana.

"I'm guessing that with the criminals either dead or in the hospital, the cops figured no one would be snooping around up here anymore, including us. So they figured it would be easy to come back for the treasure. But they didn't count on Steve being here," said Milena.

"Are you saying that you think the cops killed Steve and Butch?" asked Rosana.

But before Milena could answer, a loud bang echoed from the cave.

Rosana sighed and slumped down. She knew what the gunshot meant.

The girls stood up and ran back into the cave.

"Oh my God!" said Rosana.

Joe was slumped over sideways, the gun now by his side. Where his mouth and bottom part of this face should have been was now nothing more than a gaping hole of ooze with bits of teeth and bone fragments showing. Blood and bits of brain matter were splattered on the wall behind him.

Milena, who was usually unshakable, started to shake and said, "All this death! It's just too much for me to handle." She turned her back to Joe. She couldn't look at him or Steve's dead body anymore. "We'd better go call the police," she continued. "We need to explain to them what we saw because from the looks of things, they may think it was a gun fight between Steve and Joe that ended with both of the men dead."

"No, they won't think that" Rosana said. This time, she needed to be strong for Milena. She put her arm around Milena and the two slowly walked out of the cave as they talked. "Clearly, Joe's blood is fresh whereas Steve's blood is not. I know those cops are stupid, but they aren't that stupid," she said. "And I'm not so sure they are even on the island anymore. If Hrenek and Radic did this, they are probably long gone by now. I think it would be best if we asked to speak to the police chief."

"I agree," said Milena. "If they ask us who we are, let's tell them we are concerned citizens and we have information about new developments regarding some criminal activity."

"That sounds like a good plan," agreed Rosana.

They walked back to Milena's house. When they got there, they told Milena's parents what happened to Steve, Butch, and Joe.

"No!" Mira gasped as she put her right hand over her heart. "Steve was such a good man. I can't believe they killed him." She sobbed softly into her handkerchief as Angelo sat her down, made her a cup of tea, and gave it to her to drink to calm her down.

Although Angelo was silent, his brow was furrowed and he was deep in thought. *'Thank God the girls are unharmed,'* he thought. *'I can't believe they went back to the cave. I'm really worried and I should say something because they are putting themselves in danger. But I don't want to upset them any more than they already are.'*

"Let's call the police," was all he said.

About an hour later, there was a knock at their door. Milena answered it.

Two police officers greeted them. Officers Goran Matic and Mladen Vukovic were about ten years apart in age. The older one, Vukovic, was around 40 years old and in excellent physical shape. His sandy blonde curly hair perfectly complimented his green eyes. He sported a horseshoe mustache and had a mole on the left side of his face. The younger one, Matic, was slender but fit, and clean shaven. His straight jet-black hair, blue eyes, suave complexion, and dimples in his checks and chin made Milena swoon for a moment. She couldn't resist that twinkle in his eye. As tough as Officer Matic thought he was, he couldn't help but feel a little nervous around her.

Officer Matic spoke first. "Are you Angelo's wife?" he said sheepishly. The report said that Angelo called, and he knew Angelo had a wife. So, he was expecting a middle-aged woman to answer the door, not a young and beautiful girl.

"No. I'm his daughter. Who are you?" Milena asked point-blank.

"I'm Officer Goran Matic and this is Officer Mladen Vukovic," he paused nervously, cleared his throat and continued. "The chief asked us to check out the crime scene. He doesn't usually come out until there is a confirmed case."

"Oh. Well, what happened to Hrenek and Radic? Why didn't they come?" asked Milena.

"We don't know, miss," said Officer Matic. "They left to go on patrol, but never came back. No one knows where they are, not even their families."

Milena, Rosana, and Milena's parents exchanged worried glances. They knew exactly what happened. Rosana had forewarned them that this would happen, and she was right.

"We know what may have happened," said Angelo as he motioned for the men to come inside. "We think greed got the better of them and they went back to the cave to steal artifacts from the lost treasure the girls discovered in the cave, and then the crooked cops left the country with the loot."

"Excuse me? Did you say lost treasure?" asked Officer Vukovic. "What are you talking about? We weren't aware that anyone found treasure in the cave or anywhere else for that matter."

"Please, officers," said Angelo impatiently. "Let's get going and we can tell you all about it on the way up to the cave. I have a feeling we don't have a moment to waste."

"Wait a minute!" interrupted Milena. She turned to the officers and said, "Steve … the dead man … has several dogs at his compound. Those dogs haven't been fed for at least three days. Can we stop by the grocery store and get some dog food for them before we go up?"

"I'll tell you what, Milena," interjected her father. "Your mom and I will go up with the officers while you and Rosana get the dog food. I don't want the villagers to see any more police officers milling around. We don't need a crowd of panicked people. We will take the car and the coroner's van and drive around to the west side of the mountain. It will take a lot longer, but this way, carrying the bodies down the mountain in the stretchers will be easier."

"Okay, we will feed the dogs and meet you there," said Milena.

The two groups went their separate ways.

After purchasing the dog food at the general store, the girls headed up the mountain. When they approached the compound, they heard the dogs barking, as usual. Once at the dogs' fenced area, they opened the gate, quickly ripped open the bag of dog food, and scattered it all around. The famished dogs greedily devoured every morsel.

"That should be good for now," Milena said. "Let's go up to the cave now." They left the dogs' area and closed the gate behind themselves so the dogs wouldn't escape.

As they walked past Steve's house, Rosana noticed something. The front door to his home was ajar, and the lock was broken, just hanging out of the hole in the door. "Look at that!" she said, pointing to the door.

The girls looked at each other, wide eyed and confused. They slowly approached the front door. Milena pushed it open slightly and then called out with a trembling voice, "Hello? Is anybody there?"

Silence.

With that, she gently pushed the door open further and walked in with Rosana right behind her.

Once inside, they looked around, speechless. All the sofa cushions were slit open and the stuffing was pulled out and spewed all over the floor. Chairs were turned upside down and slit open from underneath and their stuffing was also ripped out. The kitchen cabinets were flung open and broken dishes were all over the kitchen floor. Dresser drawers were flung across the room with all their contents spilled onto the bedroom floor. The entire house was in shambles. It didn't take a genius to figure out what happened.

"What the hell?" said Milena. "Was this a robbery?" she asked Rosana as she looked around in a panic thinking that the robbers might still be in the house.

"No, this wasn't a robbery," said Rosana looking around and keeping an eye on the door. "Someone was here looking for something specific and very valuable; otherwise, they wouldn't have ransacked the place like this."

"One of the criminals must have ransacked the place looking for the drugs. But who?" asked Milena.

"Could Joe have done this before he went up the mountain?" asked Rosana. "Or was it Alex? Maybe he escaped the hospital too. But … no … it couldn't have been Joe. The door was locked and closed like normal when we passed by this morning."

"Oh my God," exclaimed Milena. "We'd better get up to the cave. What if Alex did this and now he's up in the cave? He's ruthless! My parents are up there! Let's go!" She grabbed Rosana's arm and pulled her to leave.

"Milena, don't worry. The cops are with your parents. He's outnumbered," she reassured her friend as she pulled her back into the room.

"You don't know that! What if it isn't Alex, but the drug boss and his goons? Do the cops stand a chance against them?" exclaimed Milena, wild eyed and hands waving in the air as frenzy overtook her.

"Oh damn, I didn't think of that," said Rosana. "In that case, we had better find Steve's rifles and take them with us."

They searched for the rifles and found them in the back of his bedroom closet. They each grabbed one and loaded their pockets with ammunition.

"I hope we don't have to use this," said Rosana.

"That makes two of us," echoed Milena, as they turned around toward the bedroom door.

"STOP RIGHT THERE," ordered the short husky man standing at the bedroom door. He pointed his gun at the girls. He had on a fedora hat and was smoking a fat cigar. His heavy New York accent made it clear that he was a foreigner.

Rosana and Milena gasped. They didn't expect this muscular ape-like brute standing in the doorway blocking their exit. Rosana's heart started beating faster, and she felt the skipped beats of her irregular AFib heartbeat. Milena's mouth fell open and her eyes widened with fear. She was so taken aback that she froze where she stood not knowing what to do.

"Where's Larry?" he demanded.

"Who?" Milena managed to say. "We don't know any Larry."

"Oh, ya don't, huh? Then why are yous in his house?" asked the stranger.

"There is no Larry here," said Milena. "The man who lives here is Steve."

"Okay, whatever. Where's Steve?" demanded the man.

"We don't know. We haven't heard from him in days, so we came up here looking for him," said Milena.

"Did you ransack his house?" asked Rosana timidly. "What are you looking for?"

"I told yous. I'm looking for Larry, or whatever he calls himself these days," snapped the stranger.

"Hey, Boss," yelled a man's voice from outside the house. They heard footsteps approaching and the dogs barking. "We checked…" he stopped suddenly as he saw the girls over the husky man's shoulder. "Who's the broads?" he asked in the same accent as the husky man's.

"Vito! Shud up!" said the husky man holding the gun. "Shud up and bring those rifles they're holdin' over here, and then see if there's more pieces in that there closet." He pointed in the direction of the closet behind the girls.

"Okay Boss. I was just gonna tell ya that we ain't found nothin' in the other buildings," said Vito.

"I told ya to shud up! Now get movin' and grab the ammo too," repeated the boss.

"Geez, Vinnie, why ya bein' so rude in front of these beaudiful ladies?" said Vito in his New York accent as he eyed the girls up and down.

"SHUT UP VITO!" he yelled and turned his attention back to the girls.

"I'll ask ya just once more! Where's Larry?"

Milena, finding her courage, answered, "I'm not telling you anything because I don't know where he is and I don't know who you are either."

"You're protectin' your friend, ain't ya?" As he talked, his words blended in weird sounding ways that made it difficult for the girls to understand. Milena wondered what "aintcha" meant. He continued, "There's a lot about Larry that yous don't know. Did ya know he waz a killa? I bet he didn't tell ya that he killed two of my men, did he?"

"What?" asked Milena. "No, he isn't a killer! He's a nice man who minds his own business. You have the wrong person, mister… what did you say your name was?"

"I didn't say, doll. NOW STOP STALLIN' AND TELL ME WHERE HE'S AT," shouted Vinnie angrily clenching his teeth.

"You've got the wrong man," insisted Milena. "Steve doesn't have a bad bone in his body."

"Oh, he's got ya fooled pretty good if that's what ya think," said the boss. "Did yous ever wonder why he's livin' up here on the mountain in a nothin' town? Did it ever occur to yous that he may be on the run and hidin' in this obscure little village of yours for a reason?"

Rosana couldn't believe what she was hearing. *'Surely, this is a case of mistaken identity. Steve is far from being a killer or a fugitive,'* she thought.

Milena was dumbfounded as she stood there shaking her head. "No, mister. I don't know who this Larry guy is, or what he did to you, that you had to ransack the house like this. But you have the wrong person. Steve is the sweetest, kindest man I've ever met. He's like a father to us girls," she continued.

"What makes you think that this Larry person lives here, anyway?"

"Let's just put it this way, doll," said the boss man, "I got my sources."

"Well, your sources, whoever they are, are wrong!" insisted Milena.

"Look sweetheart, my sources ain't wrong … they're never wrong! Let me tell ya the real story of your friend 'Steve' as yous call him," said the boss man. "Steve is a stool pigeon, see? He ratted out a government official, a state senata, for takin' bribes from one of our … umm … shall we say, associates? Our associate had a deal with this senata, see? The senata got a cut of the take for turnin' his head the uhtha way while our associate conducted business, ya see? You know, one hand washes the uhtha? This senata helped us move smack and crack in his state. Your 'friend' who was an undercover cop at the time, turned in the senata and testified against him in court. Larry and his cop friends were in a restaurant enjoyin' a nice lunch, ya know, when we made a hit on him. But he killed two of my men during the gun fight. The cops waz protectin' your friend, so they made it sound like my men waz killed by a rival who had it in for us, ya see? After that, Larry was put into the witness protection program because his ass waz grass, get it?"

Milena and Rosana were having a hard time taking all this in. Between his funny accent and words, and the story about Steve he was telling, they were confused. *'Could this be true?'* thought Rosana. *'There's no way on God's green earth that this could be true!'* She tried dismissing the whole story, but in her head, she kept hearing the words *'undercover cop, fugitive, witness protection. Could this be true?'* she kept asking herself.

Noticing the bewildered look on the girls' faces, Vinnie figured maybe they didn't know anything about Larry after all. They were just kids. Even if they spent a lot of time with Larry, he wouldn't have told them about this past, he reasoned.

Vinnie walked over to Milena, grabbed her arm tightly, and put the gun to her head. Milena panicked and inhaled sharply as she felt the cold steel of the gun at her temple. With a snarled upper lip he said, "I'll take your word that ya know nothin' about this, doll ... for now. But don't think that you're home free, sweetheart. My men will be watching ya and your friend like a hawk, Capisce? Now get outta here," he said. As he released her and pushed her away, she fell right into Rosana.

Milena and Rosana, with their 'deer in headlights' eyes, were too scared to do anything else but nod their heads.

They ran out of Steve's house as quickly as they could. As they ran, they noticed a few other men milling around in the other buildings on the compound.

"What do you think that was all about," asked Milena as sweat beaded up on her forehead. "Do you believe what that guy said? Do you think Steve was really an undercover cop? I can't believe this! I don't know what to believe. Do you think they were looking for drugs? I don't understand, I truly don't," she nervously rambled on.

"I don't know. I don't know what to believe. I can't imagine that it's true, but why would he make it up?" said Rosana. "That Vito guy called him 'boss' and referred to him as Vinnie. I think that was a slip-up, because the boss guy certainly didn't want to tell us his name. So, this Vinnie guy has to be either a mobster or a drug lord. Maybe they were looking for the cocaine. I don't know," replied Rosana, not wanting to believe the story she heard. But the facts were convincing her otherwise.

"Yes, that would make sense," said Milena breathing hard. "We'd better hurry and get to the cave before those men come after us. The last thing we want is for them to follow us up there."

When they arrived at the cave, they listened carefully for any signs that would indicate there were other people than their parents and the cops there. But they didn't hear anything. They turned on their flashlights and carefully entered the cave. Other than the dead bodies from earlier, there was nobody to be seen.

"Where are they?" asked Milena.

"Let's check the secret chamber," said Rosana.

Together, the girls struggled to open the chamber door. When it finally opened, they saw the cops with guns drawn, and Milena's parents, staring back at them.

"Oh, it's you! You girls scared us," said Mira. "We thought it might be one of the criminals."

Angelo chimed in, "You were right, Rosana. Radic and Hrenek were here and they took some of the gold and religious artifacts and about half the cocaine. I guess they couldn't carry any more."

The girls told the officers what happened down at Steve house.

"You should see the place," said Milena talking very fast. "They totally ransacked his house. The sofa cushions are slit, dresser drawers and clothes are thrown all over the bedroom, and they broke all the dishes in the kitchen. The entire house is in shambles."

"And there was this mobster guy inside," said Rosana talking just as fast. "He was looking for some guy named Larry. He thinks Larry is really Steve. That mobster guy, Vinnie, and another one named Vito were at the house, but other guys were on the compound too. They were searching for something and they left no stone unturned."

Milena's parents, the two officers, and the coroner watched and listened as Milena and Rosana told the story. They spoke so fast that Officer Matic made them tell the story again, this time filling in the details. As the girls retold the story yet again, he took notes frantically in his little flip note pad.

When the officer thought he had enough information for a coherent story, he walked outside to use his walkie-talkie to notify the station of what the girls told him.

"Karlo," he said to the officer on the other end, "you're going to want to get the police chief to hear this. Yes, it's that urgent. Get him quick."

Once the police chief was on the walkie, Officer Matic told him about the two dead men and the dead dog, just as the girls reported. Then he told him about the secret chamber, the treasure, the cocaine, and the crooked cops.

"What??!!" Police Chief Petrovic exclaimed. "Let me get this straight. You're telling me that there's treasure…Knights Templar treasure … in the cave? And that Hrenek and Radic stole some of the artifacts and fled with the cocaine? And we didn't know anything about this?" said the baffled police chief. "I am on my way there. Secure the area. I have to see this for myself. And don't let those girls leave. I want to question them myself. Make sure their parents are present too."

'We now have four dead people,' thought Rosana. *'Mario, Pete, and Steve were murdered, and Joe killed himself. And then there's poor Butch.'* She was distraught thinking about it and leaned against the wall of the chamber with sadness and sorrow in her heart. She felt weak and beaten. Not physically beaten, but mentally. The thought of Steve's death was too much for her heart to take. She worried as her heart palpitated faster and skipped a few beats. She could feel her irregular heart beat and she put her hand to her chest.

"Are you alright, Rosana?" asked her friend.

"Not really," replied Rosana. "It's sinking in that we will never see Steve or Butch again. This is so unfair."

"Rosana, hang in there. I was fond of Steve and Butch too, and I'm saddened by their deaths as well. But we need to focus and we need to move on. They say 'time heals all wounds' so let's look forward to the future," said Milena being strong for her friend and trying to get her friend's mind off the ordeal they were going through.

Within an hour, two more men arrived. One was the police chief, a man with an obvious mannerism of authority about him. Chief Petrovic, was a tall, older, brawny man in his fifties with black hair and hazel eyes. He walked with a slight limp. Milena assumed that his leg was hurt in the line of duty. The other man was the coroner, Zoran Jurkovic. He was medium height, slightly heavy set, and in his early fifties. His curly brown hair fell softly on his face, and were in stark contrast to his blue piercing eyes that seemed to notice every detail.

Officer Matic took the chief into the chamber to see the treasure. Again, he reiterated what Milena's parents' thought had happened to Officers Radic and Hrenek.

"This is crazy," said Police Chief Petrovic. "I gotta tell you. At first when you told me all this, I thought it was some kind of sick joke. But now after seeing this … I just can't believe this." He paused and looked around the room in awe. "And Hrenek and Radic … my God … they have disgraced our police department beyond repair. Now everyone will be suspicious of the officers in our precinct," he said. "It will take a long time to restore their trust in us."

Again, he stopped and walked around the chamber, almost in a trance. "We need to do the right thing for Steve, though," he went on. "We need to give Steve a hero's funeral. He died trying to catch those disgraced officers. We also need to call the Archaeological Museum in Zagreb to have them come out here and take a look at what's in this chamber. In the meantime, I'll put out an APB on Hrenek and Radic."

During all this, the coroner, was photographing the area and preparing the bodies for transport. Finally, it was time to load the bodies onto stretches and bring them down the mountain to the van.

Before anyone was allowed to leave, Police Chief Petrovic took everyone outside the cave and questioned Milena and her parents. He instructed Rosana to wait by the boulder, and told her he would have questions for her once they got to her parent's house.

"I know you folks are grieving and I'm sorry to have to ask you these questions, but they are important," said Chief Petrovic. "Why were you in the cave today?" he asked Milena.

"Rosana and I were concerned because we hadn't heard anything from anyone as to why the antiquities specialist hadn't come to the island. We thought that this being the discovery of the century, surely, they would come. And we also thought it was strange that no reporters showed up either. So, we went to Steve's house to find out if he had heard anything over his ham radio. But he wasn't there, so we came up here to look for him. That's when we found Steve and Butch and, eventually, Joe in the cave. So we went back to my home and told my parents. They called you guys. But before we came back up here, we went back to Steve's house to feed his dogs. When we got there this time, his place was ransacked and we had a run in with this guy Vinnie with a New York accent and his side kick Vito. We think he was either a drug kingpin or a mobster. Anyway, he was looking for someone named Larry. We kept telling him there was no Larry living there, but he insisted that Steve was Larry. Do you know anything about Steve being in the witness protection program?" Milena asked the chief.

"Ahhh, no, I don't and neither Hrenek nor Radic told me anything about any of this," said the chief, a bit dismayed and frustrated at the same time.

"What did this mobster guy, Vinnie, and his friend look like?" asked Chief Petrovic.

Milena described the boss man and his side kick Vito, along with what she saw of the other men milling around on the compound.

"What did Alex, Joe and Pete tell you that made you think this was drug related, before you actually discovered the cocaine?"

"We knew it had to be something very valuable. I thought it might be money, but Rosana said it couldn't be money because they referred to this thing as 'stuff'. She insisted that it had to be something other than money. That's when we got to thinking it was either drugs or some type of jewelry or even loose diamonds and jewels. But when we met the three men together, that's when Alex came out and said it was cocaine. He thought we took it, but we didn't. We didn't know it existed until later when we opened the door to the vault," said Milena.

"What made you think there was a vault in the first place?" asked the chief.

"We found a clue and that led us to that boulder," said Milena as she continued to tell the story of how they dug and found the stone with its etching and how Steve discovered an etching at the top of the boulder.

"When those criminals took you hostage, did they say anything that led you to believe they were involved with a drug trafficking ring, or that they were mixed up with the mafia?" asked the chief.

"No, as a matter of fact, it was what they didn't say that got us to thinking," said Milena.

"What do you mean?" asked the chief.

"Well, they weren't questioning us after we got to the camp site. They weren't trying to extract any more information from us. We thought that was strange, so we figured that they must have made contact with someone, maybe someone who would torture us for the answers. That's why Rosana was so intent on figuring out a way to escape," said Milena.

"She's a very clever girl," said the chief, "but you are both very lucky that you weren't killed. I'm sorry that Officers Hrenek and Radic put you in such danger."

"We know this mountain like the back of our hand," said Milena. "We had the advantage over them. That's the reason we were able to find our way back so quickly in the dark with only the meager light of the flashlight."

The chief asked Milena some more questions, then told her she could go while he questioned her parents.

After the chief finished with his questioning, he told everyone they could return to their homes. He then told Rosana that he was ready to drive her home so he could question her in detail in the presence of her parents.

Milena and her parents got into Angelo's car. Milena's mother was unusually quiet and looked upset. She sat in the front seat and turned her body around so she could look Milena in the eyes as she spoke. "Milena, now listen to me," she said. "You girls have had a harrowing day, not to mention the last few weeks. I am worried that the drug boss and his hit men will be coming back to find their cocaine. We want you girls to keep away from the cave. Do you understand? I don't think it's too much to ask. The police chief has everything under control."

"What about the dogs, mom?" asked Milena. "What's going to happen to Steve's dogs?"

"I don't know, dear. The police chief is handling that," said Mira.

"Did Steve have any family or relatives that you know of, mom?" asked Milena.

"I don't know. He was a very private man. That's one of the reasons he lived up in the mountain and everyone respected his privacy. No one bothered him. When he came into the village to buy his supplies, he was cordial, though he never really socialized with anyone. He just came, got his supplies, and left."

"Mom, do you think that story about Steve being in the witness protection program is true?"

"I don't know, dear. That's not the type of thing Steve would have shared with anyone. Perhaps that's why he chose to live on the mountain. I guess anything is possible," said Mira. She reached over the back of her seat and took her daughter's hand in hers. "Everything is going to be okay now. I'm sure of that."

The police chief drove Rosana home. When they arrived at the house, he informed her parents of what happened. Marko's eyes squinted half-closed as he stared at this daughter. Rosana felt like his stare was piercing right through her. Ana took Marko's hand and held it tight to get his attention and looked purposefully into his eyes. The touch of his wife's hand seemed to calm him down. He turned his attention to the chief and re-spectfully answered any questions the chief had.

Rosana was questioned next. The chief asked her the same questions that he asked Milena. After he finished questioning her, Rosana's face dropped and she looked very sad. "How sad and how unfair," said Rosana. "Steve really was the nicest man. He was always so nice to Milena and me. I think he really cared for us. I'm so sorry that he's dead. He died protecting us." She paused and took a deep breath as tears filled her eyes and rolled down her cheeks. "Had we not involved him in this damn case, he'd still be alive today."

By this time, she was crying so hard that Ana took her into her arms and hugged her in an effort to comfort her, but Rosana was beyond being comforted. She placed her head on her mother's shoulder and wept uncontrollably.

"I'm glad that he'll have a hero's funeral," said Ana, as tears rolled down her cheeks too.

7

THE MEDIA CIRCUS

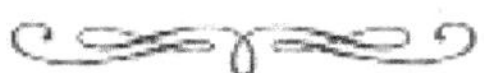

A series of muffled bell tones rang from the church bell tower whenever there was a death in the village. The death bell didn't sound like a regular church bell. The tones were lower, slower, a bit more respectful than usual bell tones. As the deep tones bellowed out, they enveloped the village in a somber embrace.

Just as the villagers had traditions for the holidays, they also had traditions for death. After a person died, the next day, the body was laid out at the home of the deceased. However, in this case, since Steve lived alone and his home was ransacked, he was laid out in the church. Typically, the villagers all attended the wake and the funeral. But news of the circumstances of Steve's death and of the discovered treasure traveled like wildfire across the island and the neighboring islands as well. As a result, people from all over flocked to the funeral. Even though they didn't personally know him, they wanted to see this now famous person who died at the hands of crooked cops while trying to protect a long-lost ancient treasure in a remote island cave. It truly was the stuff of folklore as far as the locals were concerned.

"Can you imagine?" Nino asked one of his card-playing buddies as they walked to the church to attend the wake. "The

Knights Templar treasure right here in this village, right under our noses all these centuries, and no one ever knew. Unbelievable!"

His friends shook their heads in disbelief.

Rosana and Milena kept to themselves as they walked to the church. "Nothing like this has ever happened on the island," said Rosana to her best friend. "There isn't any crime to speak of. Certainly, there are no murders and now there are four—Mario, Pete, Steve, and Butch—plus a suicide. The only criminal left standing is Alex and he is in jail."

"The village is only mourning Steve's death, though," said Milena. "He is the one who tried to stop Hrenek and Radic from stealing the lost treasure. And he's the one who lost his life trying to protect us,"

But the girls, especially Rosana, were also mourning Butch. Rosana was very fond of that dog.

When they arrived at the church, it was filled to capacity with people spilling out into the streets. As the girls approached, the large crowd parted like the Red Sea, their whispers and mumbles rising and falling in wave-like patterns, making way for the two heroines in the island's biggest adventure to reach the front of the church and view the body of their fallen friend.

The church was a kaleidoscope of colors. Flowers in every color of the rainbow filled the building from the vestibule to the alter and even up into the choir loft. There were heart shaped wreaths, sprays of flower arrangements, baskets of flowers, and a wall full of sympathy cards that the altar boys taped up. To the right of that wall were votive candle stands containing small red wax votive prayer candles that people light with a match during their prayers for the dead. Every one of them flickered today. The church had never looked so beautiful with all the flowers and the twinkling candles combined with the rays of multi-colored sunlight filtering into the church through the large stained-glass windows. It was like angels casting rays of love, comfort, and hope into the church and onto the casket.

Steve was laid out in a cherry-colored wooden casket that rested upon a stand covered with a black cloth. On the floor next to Steve's casket was a much smaller wooden casket in which Butch was laid out. This was highly unusual, but the priest made an exception since Milena and Rosana told him about the special relationship Steve and Butch had, and in light of how the dog was shot defending Steve. Butch's casket was closed, but Steve's was open. He was dressed in a navy-blue suit and white shirt with a matching tie that the girls found in his closet. They also found a detective's badge in his closet, which they polished and pinned to his suit to pay homage to his police officer status in the New York police department.

As far as anyone knew, Steve had no family, and the girls were the closest friends he had. Milena and Rosana instinctively took on the role of his family as they stood next to the coffin while the line of people passed by the coffin to pay their respects. Most of the people also expressed respect to the girls by either shaking their hand, putting their hand on the girls' shoulders, or saying a few encouraging words to the girls. Rosana and Milena held back their tears and dutifully thanked everyone for coming and for their well wishes. Once the line of people started slowing down, they took the opportunity to pay their own respects to Steve. They knelt on the kneeling bench in front of the coffin and said a silent prayer for their dear friend.

'Oh, dear Steve,' thought Rosana. *'How I miss you already. I promise you that I will do my best to take care of your family of dogs and bring honor to your name. Doing the right thing and trying to protect us is what caused your death, and for that, I'll never forgive myself. Rest in peace, my dear friend.'*

Milena had similar thoughts. '*Steve, I'm so sorry that we in-volved you in this mess. I know you cared for us; otherwise, you wouldn't have gone up to the cave to capture the crooked cops and you'd still be alive today. God rest your soul.*'

After the girls paid their respects to Steve, they stood up and left the church. They were emotionally drained and couldn't talk to one more person.

"Wow, look at all these people," said Milena as they walked through the hordes of people. "For someone who people thought of as a hermit, he sure does have a lot of people coming to pay their respects."

"I know. I was expecting that there would be a lot of people, but I never imagined this many," replied Rosana. "There are people here from other villages and even from other islands. This is huge as it's being carried over the TV stations as well," she said with quivering lips and tear-filled eyes. "How many people do you think are here?"

"Oh, I don't know. I'd say about 500 – 600, including the media," replied Milena.

— — —

In truth, thousands of people flocked to the island; they just weren't in the same exact place at the same time. There was the expected media from TV, newspapers, and magazines. But over-all, there were just too many people for the police force to control.

When the antiquities curator from Zagreb, Mr. Antovic, ar-rived, he requested that, as per protocol, the cave entrance be corded off and the cave guarded around the clock. They em-ployed several police departments from other islands to take turns guarding the cave entrance as well as the hole in one of the back chamber's ceilings that birds and bats used as their entry to the cave.

The antiquities curator and several other antiquities specialists from around the world swarmed the cave and began their scientific analysis in authenticating some of the pieces from the treasure trove to validate it was the Knights Templar treasure. All of them were examining and categorizing the pieces of gold, silver, jewels, rare artifacts, etc. that were in the cave. In addition, other staff members came and went at various times of the day. Once a few pieces were validated, they started the process of crating the massive find and labeling it for transport back to the Archaeological Museum in Zagreb where the process would continue.

"The activity to fully categorize the find may take several months or up to several years to fully complete," Mr. Antovic told the media when he saw the treasure for the first time.

Then there were the adventure travelers, the crime buffs, the looky-loos, or as the police referred to them, the gawkers. They were everywhere and all they did was get in the way. The police constantly chased them away from the cave area. They served no purpose except to satisfy their own curiosity and make pests of themselves.

"People, people, listen!" yelled Officer Vukovic in his most authoritative voice. "I'm only going to say this once. You are to leave the area of the cave. You're NOT allowed to cross the yellow crime scene tape that was setup a little further down the mountain. If you get caught up here again, you will be arrested. Is that clear?"

This was a constant event several times a day as different groups of people ignored the crime scene tape and made their way to the cave, only to be turned away by the officers on duty. But there weren't enough officers to station at both the cave entrance and further down where they installed the crime scene tape.

The media crowd had problems of their own. Because the villages on the island, though picturesque, were ancient and built centuries before cars were invented, the roads were narrow and winding donkey, and many were unpaved. The big vans filled with equipment didn't stand a chance maneuvering the paths, especially in villages such as Kali, which was built on the side of a steep hill. Some of the vans got stuck, jammed, or squished between two buildings on opposite sides of a narrowing road, with no way out. The only solution was when kind townspeople attached rope to the van's rear axle and then pulled it out backwards with the help of another vehicle. The locals had a good time watching all this unfold as they hung out from the windows of their homes, giggling or laughing at the sights.

"These dumb people! Don't they see that the car won't fit down this street?" shouted one neighbor to another out of her window while both of them delighted in the entertainment.

"Who needs television when we can just look out our window and be entertained?" said the other neighbor in delight.

The arrival of hordes of outsiders and invasion of the villages, especially Nevidane, caused great commotion not just to the people of the village, but also to the animals. With all those vehicles on the roads making their way in an unfamiliar place, they often ran off the road and scared the farm animals and farmers. The usually quiet and peaceful area was now a cacophony of donkeys braying, chickens squawking with feathers flying, and farmers yelling at the drivers of the vehicles while jumping out of the way.

Perhaps the worst part was the level at which the media inundated the villages. There wasn't an available motel, bed and breakfast, or vacation apartment rental anywhere on the island.

Some reporters found accommodations on Ugljan, which was larger than Pasman and the next island northwest of Pasman. The Zdrelac bridge connected the two islands, so reporters could drive their cars between the two islands. But, those who found a hotel room on the mainland were forced to take the car ferry to the island, which was now overflowing with newspaper and television reporters and their entourage of camera men, makeup artists, and trucks.

"These reporters are having a field day," said Rosana as they looked around at all the TV trucks that barely fit into the narrow streets.

"Of course," said Milena. "This is the biggest story of the century."

"Yes, between the murders, suicide, gun fights, treasure discovery, cocaine, and drug lords, it's a sensational story," said Rosana. "Their ratings will all sky rocket and they're milking it for all it's worth."

Various reporters setup interviews with the girls, the police chief, the police officers, the girls' parents, the museum curator, the urgent care medic, the coroner, and even some of the villagers. They didn't leave a stone overturned. If an animal or boulder could talk, they would have interviewed them as well.

"This is sensationalism in its highest form," said Rosana. "It's shameful and Steve wouldn't have liked it one bit."

"Yes, a media circus is what it is," replied Milena in disgust. "I'm sure Steve wouldn't approve of any of this. The only good thing to come out of this is that total strangers are sending money for the dogs to ensure they don't get put down."

In addition to the interviews, the girls and their parents had invitations to appear on news and talk shows from just about every corner of the world, which their parents immediately turned down. They wanted to return to their former life and wanted the media to disappear. This was bigger than anyone had imagined.

The faces of the two police officers turned criminals, Hrenek and Radic, who fled with the treasure and some of the cocaine, were plastered all over the TV, newspapers, and internet news sites.

"Those corrupt cops are international fugitives. What country would allow them entry after this kind of publicity?" asked Milena.

"It serves them right," said Rosana. "I hope they catch the bastards, lock them up and throw away the key. Better yet, I hope they get the electric chair for killing Steve and Butch."

— — —

The following day was Steve's funeral. And just as Police Chief Petrovic promised, it was a hero's funeral.

The funeral service began in the church. Father Petar, who had been the island priest as far back as anyone could remember, wore the customary black funeral vestment during Steve's funeral service. The funeral set comprised of the black vestment worn by the priest, with gold embroidery on the back and shoulders that looked like an inverted peace sign without the circle, and a gold embroidered cross at the junction of the peace sign design. The cloth on the table top on which the casket was placed also had that design. The priest said the traditional mass for Steve and then talked about his bravery in attempting to capture the rogue cops.

"As you may know by now, Steve was an undercover police detective in the United States. He was instrumental in bringing down political drug corruption in New York. He was responsible for the jailing of a major political figure and members of a drug mob consortium. Then he was placed into a witness protection program. Steve chose Croatia as his new home, as he had visited our country before and fell in love with our culture and people," said the priest.

"True to his professional calling, Steve never hesitated to help anyone in trouble, and he saved Milena and Rosana from certain death. Now, while Butch wasn't the partner police K-9 dog that Steve had in the United Stated, Butch was just as much a trained police dog and partner as any in the police department. He laid his life down to protect Steve, which is more than is expected from a human partner, and he would have succeeded had it not been for the ruthless rogue police officer who shot and killed him," continued the priest. "He deserves to be buried in the same grave as Steve."

The priest paused. But the church was not silent. Echoes of softly crying people and low murmurs rippled through the air.

"At this time," continued the priest, "if anyone would like to come up and say a few words, please feel free to do so."

With that Rosana and Milena walked up to the altar, did a quick knee bend, made the sign of the cross on their chests, and then stepped up to the dais and began their eulogy. Because they knew the coverage of the funeral would be worldwide, they decided to do the eulogy in both Croatian and English. Milena started the eulogy in Croatian while trying to control her voice from crackling.

"Steve was a kind and caring man who was always ready to lend a helping hand to anyone who needed it. Many people thought he was a hermit, but he really wasn't. But now we all know why he was such a private man. He loved our country and he learned our language. He was a true friend to Rosana and me. And he was a friend of the family too. Steve was well read and had a collection of masterpiece literature as well as music. If you got to know Steve, I'm sure you would have liked him, as he was a likable and sincere guy," said Milena.

She paused to allow Rosana to repeat it in English. Then she continued.

"Steve had no family, as far as anyone knows. So, in a way, we all, along with his dogs, were his family, his new family, here on the island. Steve was one of the kindest people we've ever met. Very accommodating and a second father to us girls. Steve's family of well-trained dogs protected Steve from criminals that might have found out where he lived and intended to harm him, as was the case of the mob boss that found out where he lived. Steve, we think about you fondly and always will. You have not been forgotten and never will be. We hold you close within our hearts and there you will remain, to walk and guide us throughout our lives until we meet again."

This time, Rosana spoke in Croatian and Milena translated to English.

"Even though Steve didn't like to be the center of attention, he had an undeniable impact on the community. If he was here with us today, he wouldn't want us to share grief and sorrow. Instead, his desire would be to focus on the happy memories and joyful experiences we shared over the years. I can't imagine how empty it will feel to spend time on the mountain without Steve greeting us each time we come up. Our friendship was built on that mountain. Steve and his dogs became part of our lives and family. With his death, Steve is leaving behind a legacy of kindness, compassion, and generosity. We miss you, Steve. God rest your soul."

It was all she could say. She could no longer keep her voice from crackling as her eyes welled up with tears. So they both slowly walked back to their seats.

During the service, the girls heard many people sniffling and saw them wiping their eyes. It seemed that maybe Steve touched more lives than the girls knew. After the girls were back in their seats, Father Petar blessed Steve, closed the coffin cover, and then blessed the coffin. After that, all the people, most of them dressed in black, made a procession following the priest, the large ornate cross that one of the altar boys carried raised high in the sky, a full-size Croatian flag that one of the village men carried, and of course, the coffins. In keeping with police tradition, police officers decked out in their dress blues served as pall-bearers and carried Steve and Butch to their final resting place in the cemetery at the edge of the village. A large Croatian flag was draped over the top of the casket. And out of respect for Steve's American heritage, an American flag was also draped over the casket.

As they walked in the front of the procession line, Milena and Rosana cried. They cried for their dear friend who lost his life looking out for them. They cried for their own lives that had been turned upside down so suddenly. They cried to release the despair … the fear … the stress … and all the pent-up emotions they had stifled in the midst of the recent adventure that they honestly wished had never happened. They also cried for Steve's dogs. They wondered what would become of them.

The girls knew that those dogs meant everything to Steve, so they insisted that the dogs be allowed to join the procession to the cemetery. Some of the villagers objected to having animals at a funeral and even thought it was disrespectful and sacrilegious. Surprisingly, the priest allowed it since the dogs were Steve's only family, for all intents and purposes. So Rosana, Milena, and Milena's father each led one leashed dog in the procession.

Marko was one of the people who objected to the dogs. He couldn't be bothered with them. He thought of them as vile creatures and a disgrace to have at a funeral. "Having dogs at the funeral is disrespectful to Steve and to the religion," he said. But there was nothing he could do about it since the priest approved it.

The dogs walked quietly with their heads facing forward and their tails slowly bobbing side to side. Rosana and Milena knew the dogs were grieving Steve's death as much as they were. As the dogs walked with them, they would occasionally let out a whimper, a cry that indicated to Rosana that they were mourning. Dogs have a way of knowing when a person is sick, dying, or dead. Rosana thought it was the body language and different scents that only dogs can smell that tells them that, and she was right. "Steve's dogs are so smart," Rosana whispered to Milena. "Even though they have never been to the village or to a funeral, they know this is a serious and solemn matter," said Rosana to Milena.

The procession solemnly led to the walled cemetery at the edge of town. Directly in front of them, just past the iron gate, was a small chapel where families gathered to pray for their dearly departed family members. Just past the cemetery was the Adriatic Sea. The property to the right of the cemetery was lined with tall thin cypress trees and there was a place in the grass where one could sit and mediate or have a snack in the warm sun as they enjoyed the beautiful clear sea views of the Adriatic. The land to the left of the cemetery was being cleared for future graves as the old small cemetery was already overcrowded.

At the grave site, father Petar said a short prayer and then the caskets were slowly lowered into the grave. He then stepped aside to let people step forward, one by one, take a carnation from the pile of flowers that was laid beside the grave, and drop a single carnation into the grave on top of the caskets.

Never before this day had there been so many people in the tiny cemetery. Now, with the publicity of the events that occurred, the world would know where the island of Pasman was located and they would learn to pronounce Nevidane (Nevi-jon-e), the name of the village where it all happened. As the girls and their families left the cemetery, the press inundated them with questions, shoved mics in their faces, and snapped photos at will. The police officers did their best to keep the press from harassing the girls and their parents, but it wasn't enough as the press far outnumbered the police personnel.

"Can you tell us how you're all feeling right now?" one of the reporters asked them.

"Do you have any ideas on the whereabouts of Officers Hrenek and Radic?" another asked.

"You damn inconsiderate fools," said Marko as he pushed away the mics the reporters shoved at them.

"Leave us in peace to mourn our friend and hero Steve," said Rosana in English with tears rolling down her cheeks.

Milena and her parents also were greatly irritated at the media for not being more respectful at Steve's funeral.

"I'll sure be glad when this is all over," said Milena.

After the funeral, Angelo invited Marko, Ana, and Rosana to their house for refreshments. Mira served the traditional fare of prosut, goat cheese, seasoned olives in olive oil, home baked Italian style bread, pastries, coffee, and wine to her guests in honor of Steve. They sat around the large kitchen table with the girls on one end chatting amongst themselves while the parents held their own conversation.

"They can't seem to get enough," said Rosana about the media. "I've even heard talk that they want to do follow up stories and do a mini-series of exposés on the Dalmatian islands. I think it's just an excuse for them to stay here and party."

"Oh great!" said Milena. "We'll never get rid of them. I heard a few of them talking, and they are just in love with the Dalmatian islands, the sea, and especially the food. I overheard some reporters talking and they said that everything tastes better here, which makes sense since our foods are all organic."

"The priest gave a wonderful service for Steve," said Mira, interrupting the girls' conversation. "And you girls both did phenomenal jobs with the eulogies. I'm very proud of you both, especially since you said the eulogies in both English and Croatian," she said smiling. She stood up from her seat, walked over to the girls, and hugged them both.

"She's right," said Angelo as he looked at the girls. "We are proud of you both." He raised his wine glass in the air.

"Yes, I agree," said Marko as he raised his glass to show solidarity. Everyone at the table followed his lead and raised their glasses as well.

"To Rosana and Milena … the two bravest girls I know," said Angelo.

"Salut!" everyone chanted in unison.

Rosana blushed. *'Gee,'* she thought. *'Maybe my father is finally realizing that I'm not a child anymore, but an adult. I sure hope so because I'd be much happier if he did.'*

— — —

The media frenzy lasted a couple more weeks. After that, everyone settled back down to their normal daily life. Maybe normal wasn't the right word as all their lives had been changed by the events that happened. But life went on and for the people of Nevidane … in their 'new normal.'

8

STEVE'S LEGACY

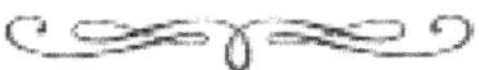

A few weeks later, after the funeral and as the media slowly trickled out of town, things started to calm down. Marko left to get back to his merchant marine job on the ship. Before he left, he sternly instructed Rosana to heed her mother and stay away from the cave. He told her he didn't want to hear that she's running around the countryside looking for trouble and making her mother's life miserable with worry.

GOOD RIDDANCE,' thought Rosana. *'I hope you don't come back until I'm legally allowed to do as I please and don't need to hear your BS anymore.'*

The girls, Angelo, Mira, and Ana took turns going up the mountain to tend to the dogs, and Angelo took the dogs hunting with him on a few occasions. However, going up and down the mountain to care for the dogs every day was exhausting. They had to come up with a better plan. And as painful as it was, the girls decided it was time to clean up Steve's place and figure out what to do with his belongings, and of course, the dogs.

They took on the smallest tasks first. They went through his clothes and picked out the ones in better condition, which they gave away to relatives, friends, and some of the less fortunate families in the village. They gave the remainder of his clothing to a company that collected all sorts of items to help out people in under developed countries. They saved some of the books and music, and gave the rest of it to libraries in Zadar.

As for the furnishings, they kept most of the items that were not destroyed when the criminals ransacked the house.

"I was thinking that with this compound, it's a shame that someone doesn't buy it and turn it into a resort," said Milena. "Steve really did a great job renovating some of the buildings, and it wouldn't take much effort for someone to come in and finish the work."

"Yes, especially since there are no hotels or motels on this island. But strangely enough, I heard rumors that they are going to be building a vegetarian hotel … Croatia's only vegetarian hotel … called Hotel Korinjak and a health spa called Nirvana on the tiny island of Iz … the land time forgot," said Rosana. "Tourism has really taken off here and the best we have to offer is someone's house that has been converted to a private bed and breakfast setup. A resort style facility would be so beneficial for this island if they want to compete in the tourism industry."

"Well, I think keeping the furnishings, for now, is a good idea. It might help sell the place," said Milena.

With that, they started to slowly examine all of Steve's other possessions, hoping they could decide what to do with each individual piece. It was a very time-consuming process because some of the things that Steve collected were unfamiliar to the girls. So, they researched each item to get an idea of its value.

"My goodness, I never realized how much money Steve invested in this ham radio set up," said Milena. "There's a lot of money tied up just in his ham radio stuff."

"Yep, just look at that banjo clock on the wall. I researched it in this antique clock book I found on his bookshelf. According to the book, it's a Simon Willard & Son stencil front presentation banjo clock circa 1830, and it's worth almost twenty thousand dollars," gasped Milena.

"WOW! Really?" said Rosana, wild eyed in surprise.

"Well, we've been at this for over a week now. I don't know about you, but I have to take a break from cleaning up. Can we just take a few days off before continuing?" asked Milena.

"Sure, I'm pretty overwhelmed myself," answered Rosana.

Several days later, the girls met at the Sovinje restaurant in Tkon for lunch.

"How's it going with Goran?" asked Rosana.

"Great actually," replied Milena. "We had a few dates already and his family invited me to their house for dinner.

"Yes, you did tell me you were going to meet the family. How did it go?" asked Rosana.

"They are very down to earth folks. I like them," replied Milena.

"That's wonderful. That's a sure sign that things are moving forward. I'm so happy for you," said Rosana.

"Thanks, how about you and Ivan?" asked Milena.

"Oh, I don't know. I'm thinking of cutting him loose," answered Rosana. "The other day we went to the beach and instead of him focusing on me, he was ogling the other girls. That's embarrassing, and I don't think he'll ever change."

"Geez, I'm sorry to hear that," said Milena.

"It's okay. Better that I find out now instead of after we're married," she said with a chuckle.

In an effort to change the subject and get Rosana's mind off Ivan, Milena started to reminisce.

"I'll never forget how we stumbled upon Steve's Will," she told Rosana as they drank their coffee. "Had we not volunteered to clean up the mess the criminals made after they ransacked Steve's house, we'd never have found his Will."

"And, you and Goran might never have discovered one another. I knew he liked you when he insisted on helping to clean up. Isn't that where he gave you your first kiss?" asked Rosana smiling.

"Yes, and it was quite the surprise. Me all covered with dust and sweat and looking like a hag from cleaning up Steve's place, to have him plant a big kiss on my lips so unexpectedly. He said I was talking too much so he kissed me to shut me up for a minute," said Milena giggling.

"And then you knew he felt the same way about you as you did about him. That's rather romantic, don't you think?" asked Rosana.

"Maybe, in an offbeat weird way," said Milena still smiling. Then, as her smile faded, she zoned out into her own private thoughts.

— — —

Milena vividly remembered how everything was broken into at Steve's compound. Sofas and chairs were slashed with the stuffing thrown all over the floor. Dishes from the kitchen cabinets littered the kitchen floor, books were flung from the bookcases in the den, and dresser drawers in the bedroom were thrown across the room with clothes spewed everywhere. There wasn't a room in the house that the drug bosses didn't destroy in their search for the cocaine that wasn't even in Steve's house.

The girls cleaned everything up and sewed up as much of the torn living room furniture as they could reasonably salvage. The rest was taken away by Angelo and several men from the village, and left on the side of the main road that ran the length of the island. From there, a sanitation truck picked the pieces up and disposed of them in the dump.

As Milena was cleaning Steve's bedroom, and putting the drawers back into the dresser, she saw a large manilla envelope taped to the bottom of one of the dresser drawers. Milena opened it. "Last Will and Testament" were printed across the top. She began to read the papers.

"I, Lawrence Marshall, also known as Steven Novak, being of sound mind and body, not acting under duress or undue influence, and fully understanding the nature and extent of all my property and of this disposition thereof, do hereby make, publish, and declare this document to be my Last Will and Testament, and hereby revoke any and all other wills and codicils heretofore made by me."

As she read it, her hands shook and her eyes grew wider. "I devise and bequeath my property, both real and personal and wherever situated, to Rosana Babic and Milena Ribar." In the Will, Steve explained that he saw in the girls his own youth, and that they made him smile and brought excitement back into his life. He further stated that since he didn't have any children of his own, they were like his surrogate daughters. They were the reason he woke up every morning. They, along with his dogs, gave him a reason to live. He left them the compound and all its contents to do with as they pleased.

Rosana walked into the room just as Milena finished reading the Will. She was both smiling and crying at the same time.

"What's the matter Milena?" asked Rosana. "Why are you crying?"

Milena didn't answer. Instead, she handed Rosana the document. Rosana read it and she too started to weep.

"I never knew we made such an impact on his life," said Rosana wiping the tears from her face.

"I know," said Milena through teary eyes. "I knew he liked us because he was always so kind and so glad to see us. But I didn't realize how lonely he really was. I don't think anyone really did. They thought he was just a hermit."

"But he was so much more than that," observed Rosana. "Look at all the great literary works we found on his bookshelves like Anna Karenina, To Kill a Mockingbird, The Great Gatsby, and Don Quixote. And look at all the classical music we found by Bach, Beethoven, Mozart, and Strauss. He was a cultured and worldly man," said Rosana.

"One of the boxes we found contained documents that said he was in the witness protection program from the United States," said Milena. "It says that he gave state's evidence about some high-ranking government official being involved in corruption with drug trafficking. That's why he was in seclusion here on a little-known island. That's also why he had such well-trained dogs. They were his alarm system as well as his defense team."

"I guess that drug lord that ransacked this place was telling the truth about Steve after all. Now that I know more about him, I feel sorry that we weren't better friends to him," said Rosana. "We should have invited him to dinner and made him feel part of our families. He was always so nice to us."

Rosana took the manilla envelope Milena was still holding so she could put the Will back inside. "Wait a minute," she said as she opened the envelope. "There's another piece of paper in here." She pulled it out and read it.

"What does it say?" asked Milena eagerly.

"Oh my God!" she exclaimed. "Steve left us five hundred thousand dollars in US currency. The note says that he never opened a bank account for fear that he'd need to leave the country in a hurry. But this note tells us exactly where to find the money," she said crying.

With that Goran came storming into the room holding up a white envelope ready to blurt out his news when he saw the girls crying.

"Was it something I said?" he asked in jest, trying to lighten the mood. "What's with the tears?"

Milena explained that she found Steve's Will and what it said.

"You should be happy," said Goran, "not crying. But what would you do with this old place anyway?"

"We're crying because he died. He was like a father to us and we miss him," said Milena a little annoyed that Goran didn't understand why they were crying.

"I know, but I still think you should be celebrating his life and not mourning his death anymore. I'm sure he wouldn't want to see you in such pain anymore," said Goran. "It would make him very happy that you're taking care of his place and his dogs."

"Speaking of dogs," said Rosana, "we still don't know what to do with them. We want to keep them together because they are family, but we can't keep going up and down the mountain all the time to tend to them and we can't keep them at either of our houses. Do you have any ideas?"

"Well, there are three of us and there are three dogs. Why can't we each take one home until we figure out what to do with them. This way you don't have to keep coming back up the mountain all the time," said Goran.

"That's brilliant!" said Rosana will a huge smile of relief on her face.

"Yes, I agree," said Milena. "If we each take one dog, it won't be so overwhelming. Thank you for coming up with that idea and for helping us clean up."

Goran once again held up the white envelope he was carrying. His eyes twinkled and he had a big smile on his face as if he had a secret he was dying to share. He fanned the envelope slowly back and forth and said, "I have good news!"

"Well, what is it?" asked Milena.

"I got a promotion! I'm now Sargent Goran Matic," he said proudly with a big grin.

"CONGRATULATIONS!" yelled Milena and Rosana in one voice.

"Oh honey, I'm so proud of you," said Milena giving Goran a kiss. "I'm taking the three of us to that little restaurant in Zadar that we all love for a celebratory dinner tonight."

"Oh, I think that's wonderful news Goran. Milena why don't you and Goran have a romantic celebration dinner with just the two of you. You both deserve it," Rosana offered.

"WHAT? No, Rosana. You're family. You're like the sister I never had, and you need to be there. It won't be the same without you. Right Goran?" said Milena.

"Absolutely," said Goran. "And I don't want to hear any more nonsense like that. The two of you are attached at the hip and I have no intention of changing that."

Rosana smiled and said, "Thank you both. I'd love to help you celebrate."

— — —

About six months later, Rosana saw an article in the newspaper that showed a picture of the two policemen who hauled off some of the treasure. She immediately telephoned Milena and asked her if Goran had any additional news regarding what she read in the newspaper. Milena told her that he did and that she would meet her at their favorite café, Kriva Smokva, down by the water.

When they met at the café, Rosana wasted no time asking Milena about the new developments.

"So, what does Goran know about what happened to Hrenek and Radic?" Rosana asked anxiously.

"Yes," said Milena, "but first let me tell you about the drug lords. That's something that wasn't in the papers. Goran said that they found Vinnie and Vito! The police chief actually found them by accident. The chief was on the car ferry going to the land office in Biograd to settle some personal issues regarding his parcels of land when he spotted two men who looked totally out of place. They had on these spiffy suits. One of them had a fedora hat too and smoked a cigar. Who wears a suit and fedora hat on the island?" she said laughing.

"So, he decided to take a closer look. He was convinced that they were the same men that we described as the boss man and his side kick. So, the chief phoned ahead to the Biograd police to meet him at the port. As the ferry approached the port, the two men got back into their car and started to drive off the ferry. As soon as they turned the corner to get onto the main street leading out of the port, they were blocked by a barricade of patrol cars and officers standing outside their cars, crouched behind open car doors, with their guns drawn. They made the men get out of the car, handcuffed them, and took them down to the police station for questioning. They were immediately thrown into the holding cell because their U.S. passports had their actual first names, though the last names were fake. But the police were able to ascertain that they were, in fact, the notorious drug lords from New York based on the pictures the New York police faxed over."

Rosana's heart jumped for joy. "That's a huge relief. Now we don't have to worry about those guys bothering us anymore."

"What about Alex," asked Rosana. "Any news about him?"

"Oh yes," said Milena. "Alex was escorted back to a prison in Germany. He was wanted there for illegal drug trafficking. Surprise, surprise! That's all Goran knows so far."

"That puts my mind at rest," said Rosana with a smile on her face.

"What is it that I know so far?" asked Goran smiling as he walked toward them to join them at the table.

"Oh, my goodness! I didn't expect to see you here. What a pleasant surprise," said Milena now standing to give her boy-friend a hug.

Goran hugged her and then planted a wet kiss on her lips. "I'm glad I spotted you here. I was looking for you because I have an update on those cops," said Goran. "Hi Rosana. How are you doing?" he asked as he sat down in the empty chair next to Milena.

After Goran and Rosana exchanged pleasantries, Rosana impatiently waited for Goran to give them an update. "The newspaper article said that the men in the picture were the ex-cops who pulled off the treasure heist on the island, but it didn't get into the nitty gritty of what happened to them other than that they were found dead in the streets of Caracas. Do you know what happened?" asked Rosana.

"Well, apparently, they thought they could go to Venezuela to sell the sacred artifacts," said Goran. "Seems like the idiots weren't keeping up with the news, and even so, are they really that stupid that they thought they could fence sacred artifacts without anyone asking any questions?"

"I guess they thought they were far enough away that no one would know who they were or what they did, especially in an economically depressed country, the poorest in Latin America," said Milena. "Maybe that's why they picked Venezuela."

"Probably, but they picked the wrong country," said Goran. "Venezuela is a very dangerous place to be right now. The blundering idiots actually said the artifacts were in their families for centuries and that they were in the antiquities business working with various Archaeological Museums, including the one in Zagreb. Of course, we know that was a big fat lie." He chuckled and then continued. "According to Hrenek's wife, she told the police chief that her husband was killed in Venezuela, which coincides with the article. But how that happened is the interesting part. It seems like they sold the cocaine in Amsterdam before they left for Venezuela, as per his wife. And though drug use is legal in the Netherlands, it only applies to small quantities of soft drugs like marijuana and hallucinogenic mushrooms for personal use. Hard drugs like cocaine, LSD, morphine, and heroin are prohibited, but the idiots didn't know that. However, as in any country, if you want to find the people who sell or buy hard drugs, you don't have to look far."

Rosana and Milena sat at the edge of their seats, taking in every word.

"Also, according to his wife, Hrenek told a drug kingpin in Amsterdam, their first stop, that they needed to sell the cocaine in order to raise funds for her cancer treatments, but she doesn't have cancer. Can you believe that? Though, I'm sure they didn't tell the drug lord about the treasure. They actually needed the money to get to Venezuela, and also to buy designer suits to look the part of rich antiquities brokers in order to give the impression that they were legit. His wife told the chief that once the cocaine was sold, Hrenek and Radic were swimming in money. He sent her money to buy first class airplane tickets to Venezuela for herself and their children. However, when she got to Venezuela, he wasn't at the airport to meet her," said Goran. "Seems the police found his dead body in the street, which is typical for kidnapped victims in Venezuela. Her son, who had taken Spanish courses at the university, was able to find out what happened. Apparently, when the crooks got to Venezuela, they were able to connect with a general in the army. He was looking to invest in gold and rare artifacts because the Venezuelan bolivar was worthless. He had millions in U.S. dollars stashed away in bank accounts in tax haven countries such as the Cayman Islands."

"Wow!" exclaimed Rosana unable to believe what she was hearing. Her heart was racing as she took in the news.

"The general paid the ex-cops a couple million dollars in U.S. currency in exchange for the gold and artifacts, which were actually priceless,' continued Goran. "But to the two ex-cops, a million each was mind blowing, so they took it. They were so thrilled with themselves that they celebrated for days flashing money around nightclubs and bars like it was water. This led to their kidnapping in Venezuela, which is notorious for kidnapping rich tourists as well as wealthy citizens. The idiots didn't want to part with any of the money, so after being tortured and still not divulging where the money was, the kidnappers finally killed them both and left their bodies in the street."

"Wow! That's some story," said Rosana wide eyed at the stupidity of the rogue cops. "Greed got them yet again. Just like I said it would."

"Karma is a bitch," agreed Milena. "They were full of themselves. They thought they were untouchable, and they got what they deserved," she said with a smile on her face.

"Yes, live by the sword and die by the sword," said Rosana with a satisfied look on her face and a beam in her eye. "This chapter in our lives is behind us … finally."

After Goran finished his cup of coffee, he bid the girls farewell as he had to get back to work.

Goran hugged Milena and told her he would he see her tonight. They kissed and he left.

"You're a lucky girl, Milena," said Rosana. "It's pretty clear that he loves you very much."

"Yes, I think I'm pretty lucky too. But, so is he, you know? I'm not exactly chopped liver," she said snickering.

"No, of course not. You guys make a great couple," said Rosana. "I wish I had someone like that."

"Oh, but you do, don't you?" asked Milena. "What about Ivan?"

"As I told you before, I'm not sure he is the marrying type," said Rosana a little down-hearted.

"What do you mean?" asked Milena with a puzzled look on her face.

"I told you already. Ivan has a roving eye," replied Rosana. "I want someone who only has eyes for me, like you and Goran. I never see Goran eying other women."

"Oh, Rosana, I'm so sorry. I didn't realize it was that serious. So, what are you going to do?"

"I'm going to state dating other men. I'm not going to be one of those women who has regrets later."

"Good for you," said Milena. "I know someone who'd be perfect for you," she said smiling.

"Now, Milena, don't you start trying to play matchmaker. It's bad enough my mom is doing that," she said with a smile on her face.

As Milena took another sip of her coffee, she asked, "And Rosana, do you remember that treasure map we found taped to the bottom of one of Steve's dresser drawers?"

"Yes, of course. How can I forget a map embossed on a silver sheet of paper? Do you think it's real?" replied Rosana.

"YES! Absolutely it's real. Why would anyone emboss a fake map on a pure silver sheet of paper?" said Milena.

"One of these days we can do some more research on that map and see what it's all about. Right now, we still have a lot of work to do," said Rosana hoping Milena wouldn't bring up that map again anytime soon.

- 9 -

A New Life

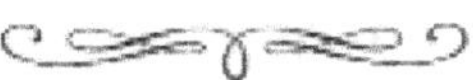

It was four years later, and Milena and Rosana were cleaning up after the large party they threw last night to celebrate their 20th birthdays. They were born in the same month, so they always celebrated their birthdays together. But this year the celebration was a little sweeter, because it was also the two-year anniversary of their business, the 'Dalmatian Paradise Resort.' That's where they threw the party to celebrate both milestones.

The resort lobby was small, but neat. The reception desk was made of brown stained wood planks, which gave it a rustic feel as soon as you walked in the door. It also had a few rustic wood chairs that Angelo stained to the same color. Ana made colorful cushions with blue and green swirls for the chairs, and she bought a large sand-colored throw rug to place over the hard wood floor. The colors reminded Rosana of the beach. There was a six-foot wooden table and stools that housed two computers for the guests.

The girls worked quickly to remove the multi-colored streamers from the ceiling, the champagne bottles from the tables, as well as the wine bottles and the glasses that were left there from the night before. They gathered up the hors d'oeuvre dishes and napkins and brought them into the restaurant to be washed.

183

They hurried with the cleanup as they were expecting their guests to be coming down for the planned daily activities.

"Milena, I've been thinking about ways to make this resort a true vacation destination. I was thinking that we should offer scuba diving lessons and a dive adventure package as our getaway packages," said Rosana.

"Are they two different packages or one?" asked Milena.

"Two. The scuba diving lessons are for people who aren't certified in open water diving yet. They would have to attend a four-hour class in the morning and pass the written quiz. Then in the afternoon they would practice dives in shallow waters by the shore. The following day, they would practice dives from the boat in water up to 30 feet deep. The dive adventure package is for experienced divers who are already certified and they would need to show us their PADI certification, or other certification card for insurance purposes, in order to get on the dive boat. They would depart with a dive master that we hire to operate the tour, and they would go diving in water 30 feet and deeper," explained Rosana. "We can even offer night dives and wreck drives if we get requests."

"That's a great idea. Let's do it!" said Milena. "We can call it the 'Dive Here, Stay Here' package. How does this sound: 'Explore the Dalmatian islands by land and by sea with a Dive Here, Stay Here package?'

"Sounds like great fun," said Rosana.

"We could turn that smaller building on the mountain into a diving gear supply shop and turn that little shack down by the water into the dive registration shop," said Milena.

"Right," said Rosana. "No one else on the island offers scuba diving lessons, nor do any of the neighboring islands, as far as I know. And, I don't think tourists would mind that the dive shop is located mid-way up the mountain. It has spectacular million-dollar views of the Adriatic and of Lover's Island. They could book day trips. Or, they could stay at the resort, go on a boat dive trip in the morning, have a boxed lunch on Lover's Island, and return their gear here."

"That's brilliant," said Milena. "But why would the tourists mind that the dive shop is located mid-way up the mountain? We spent a heck of a lot of money putting in the road that links the resort to the main road on the island so that guests could drive up here. It's not as if they have to walk. People actually don't mind the walk though. The guided hiking tours of the island we offer are very popular with the younger crowd."

"That's true, but we built the road so guests wouldn't have to lug their luggage up the mountain. Hiking is an entirely different story," Rosana said teasingly with a big smile.

"I know, I know … you're right. But you know, the Zadar archipelago day trips we offer are so popular that we need to add another sail boat and captain to run the trips. I'm also thinking we need an additional sail boat and a captain just to run the dive tours," said Milena.

"Hey, Ivan has a boat! Maybe he'd be interested in taking the job of boat captain. I'll ask him," said Rosana.

"I thought you were going to dump him," said Milena.

"Look, I know I'll never marry him. He is too much of a ladies' man and I no longer have feelings for him, so it makes no difference to me what he does with his time. But he is a good sailor and has a captain's license. That's the only reason I'm suggesting we ask him if he's interested," said Rosana. "But we'll have to advertise for a dive master. I don't know anyone who could fill those shoes." She paused.

Milena could see the wheels in her head spinning and knew Rosana was about to blurt out another idea.

"Oh!" Rosana said excitedly. "Maybe we could lease the dive shop to a dive master. He would pay for all utilities and give us a small percentage of his dive revenue as rent. Other than that, he is free to conduct business without our interference."

"I think that's a splendid idea, Rosana," said Milena. "This way, we don't have to pay him a salary. We spend a little money on renovating the shack and the small building, but we have no inventory expense."

"On second thought," said Rosana wide eyed as a different approach entered her mind, "it would be better if we charge the dive master a fixed price rent. We have no way of knowing what his dive revenue is. We'd just have to take his word for it, so it doesn't really make sense to take a percentage. He would probably tell us it's way less than it really is, and then we'd get into the situation where we would have to examine his books, but the books can be cooked, so we will never really know his true revenue. Why go through that aggravation? I think a flat rate is the better route to take."

"Okay, whatever you think is best. You're the business guru," said Milena smiling.

They continued cleaning the lobby in silence for a moment. Milena looked up and saw the small framed picture of Steve that they kept on the wall behind the front desk. She remembered the day they took that photo. It was the day Milena got a new camera from her parents. The girls went up the mountain to take some nature photos, and of course to show Steve the new camera. He posed in a Superman pose, with his legs planted firmly on the ground, his hands on his hips, his chest out proudly, and his chin high. All he needed was a cape to complete the look. Milena snapped the picture, and now it hung in the front lobby, which used to serve as Steve's parlor.

"You know," Milena continued, "we are very fortunate that Steve left his compound to us in his Will. At first, I couldn't imagine what we would do with this compound, but now with your business sense and my marketing efforts, we found a niche that needed to the filled."

"Yes, it was truly the perfect storm, in a positive way. This storm cleared the path for us to get to where we are today. None of this would have been possible if it wasn't for Steve's wishes to leave this compound to us, the extraordinary events that led up to this moment, and the media coverage of the Knights Templar treasure discovery. Nevidane has become a tourist attraction the likes of which may someday rival Zadar. Who would ever have thought that was possible?" said Rosana with a far-off twinkle in her eye.

"We don't even have to advertise," said Milena. "The news coverage put Nevidane on the map. People are coming from all over to the once unknown Friar Cave in droves now. Most come to Zadar and take day excursions to the island just to see the cave. But the travel agencies are really the ones doing all the work to promote our village just by virtue of promoting the cave … You know, we really need to offer our own cave exploration trips."

"You're right! That could be another lucrative source of revenue for us," said Rosana. "And who knows the cave better than we do?" she said laughing. "We can even add a boxed lunch, or make lunch at the restaurant part of the package. This way, after lunch, they can check out the gift shop and buy souvenirs to take back with them. It was a brilliant idea, by the way, to connect the restaurant to the gift shop."

"I do love seeing how the entire island is thriving now," said Milena. "Between our resort and all the other vacation rentals and bed and breakfasts here on the island, our little island has become a true vacation destination from all over the world. So many of the villagers are prospering. That makes me very happy."

"Agreed," said Rosana. "What's really cool is that now my mom and your parents have a role in this enterprise too. Seriously …. if we hadn't found Steve's Will when we were cleaning his place, this compound would have just slowly deteriorated and his dogs would have been put down. But now look at it. It's a beautiful thieving enterprise and his dogs are safe."

"Yes, and watching it deteriorate would have been a shame considering how much work Steve put into these old buildings," remarked Milena.

"The buildings are nicely appointed and the village is so quaint. It takes you back to another time when pirates frequented these parts. It's romantic and really very lovely," said Rosana.

"I know. You always loved this old picturesque stone village. Now you are a part owner," said Milena. "This is a perfect venture for us. If the buildings weren't so small, we could have even offered wedding packages here, but none of the buildings are large enough to host a wedding."

"We improved it a lot and I feel proud of what we did with Steve's compound," said Rosana. "I just know he is smiling down on us from heaven. I know in my heart that he approves of what we did with his place. The money he left us made it possible for us to do more renovations on the compound, convert some of the buildings to vacation rental apartments, and to start this wonderful business."

"Well, he has made me and my family very happy," said Milena as she stared at his picture with a smile that spelled satisfaction. "I know my mom is doing the job that she loves. She doesn't have to work in the fields so much anymore and break her back to put food on the table. She told me she loves cooking and baking for our guests, and that makes me happy. So, you see, this really worked out well for both of our families."

Just then, Mira came into the office. "The dogs are bathed and fed," she said a little out of breath as she pushed her hair out of her eyes with the back of her hand. "They really haven't been the same since Steve died," she said sadly. "They know Steve isn't coming back. They aren't as feisty as they were when he was alive. I feel sad that they still miss him so much."

"It's okay mom," said Milena. "At least the dogs are still here on the property and they weren't put down. They'll always have a home. I've been taking them for walks up the mountain and Dad takes them hunting with him, and they love being active. They really like being with Dad too. I think Dad has become attached to them as well. So, it's really a win-win scenario, don't you agree?"

"Yes, I suppose you're right dear," said Mira.

"How are you and Goran doing dear," asked Mira smiling at her daughter.

With that, Milena flashed the biggest smile and squirmed as if to contain a "happy dance."
"Mom, you'll never guess!" Milena squealed. "I was just going to announce the good news."
Both Rosana and Mira stopped in their tracks and looked at Milena with wide eyes, in anticipation of what they hoped she'd say next.

"Goran and I got engaged last night!" she blurted out as she held up her left hand to show them the sparkling diamond on her ring finger.

"Oh my God!" exclaimed Mira and Rosana in unison with huge smiles on their faces. Mira ran over and hugged her daughter tightly. Rosana was next to hug her best friend.

Rosana took Milena's hand in hers and admired the ring. "It's beautiful!" she said. "Why didn't you tell us sooner?"

"I wanted to wait until my mom was here," replied Milena. "It's something I wanted to share with the two most important women in my life."

"Awe, I'm so happy for you, Milena," said Rosana.

"I knew that young police officer was sweet on you the moment I met him," said Mira. "The way he looked at you as if you were the most beautiful woman he'd ever seen, and he got tongue tied when he was around you. It was a dead giveaway."

"Have you set a date yet?" asked Rosana.

"Not yet, but we aren't in a hurry," said Milena.

"We need to throw you two an engagement party," said Rosana, her mind envisioning the decorations.

"Milena, you know what story I love hearing?" said Rosana smiling and trying to relish the mood.

"Yes, yes, I know… the story of my first date with Goran," said Milena laughing. "Okay, I know it was funny and one we will tell our grandchildren someday. But you have to admit, him arranging to have fireworks go off from a barge in the sea as we ate dinner at the seaside restaurant was romantic, until the rain hit and put out the show just as it was getting started."

"Uh-huh," said Rosana as she nodded and smiled, "And then he went to see if they could salvage any of the fireworks for after the rain. But after he stepped on the barge, he tripped over a rope and went head first into the sea. Now, that's the funny part," said Rosana laughing, and Milena and Mira joined in too.

Just then, Rosana's mother came into the office.

"Did I miss something?" she asked looking around with a smiling but puzzled look on her face. "You all look so happy."

"Yes, mom," said Rosana with a big smile on her face. "Milena got engaged to Goran last night!"

"Oh my goodness! Congratulations Milena!" exclaimed Ana. "I'm so happy for you." She kissed Milena on the cheek and admired the ring on Milena's finger. She then turned to Rosana and said, "You know Rosana, Luke was asking about you. I ran into him yesterday at the market and he said he was wondering why he doesn't see you around anymore. I told him you were busy with the business and he said he was going to come up to visit you and to see what you've done with the place."

"Mom, I told you that I'm not interested in starting a relationship right now," Rosana said, slightly annoyed. "Why are you in such a rush to see me get married? It will happen in its own time."

"Okay dear, but don't get so immersed in your work that you forget about building a future and a family of your own. Work isn't everything," she said smiling. Then she quickly changed the subject and said, "I'd better get into the gift shop and start dusting before guests come down." She turned and walked toward the little gift shop. She stopped at the door and turned toward Milena with a huge smile and said, "Congratulations again, Milena," just before she existed the office.

Ana was thrilled to be working in the gift shop. She looked around the shop with pride. She started to hum a soft tune while dusting the knick-knacks on the shelves. *'Who would ever have thought this was possible? Me and my daughter working together in a business where we don't have to break our backs to earn a decent living. Looking around, I can proudly say that I, Ana, made this shop what it is today,'* she thought to herself, beaming from ear to ear.

Ana loved running the shop. She and Milena's father, Angelo, worked hard to spruce up and maintain all the buildings. Angelo painted the doors and window frames in lively colors of green and blue, and made colorful signs for all the buildings. He also planted native plants and flowers around the compound and he did all the repairs. Ana made café curtains for the restaurant and she made and sold handmade doilies that the tourists snapped up like hot cakes. She kept the gift shop clean and organized, and well stocked with a variety of popular souvenirs. In her down time, she created small water color paintings of local seaside and mountain scenes that guests loved and bought up faster than she could paint them.

'And it's so nice working with Mira,' she thought happily. *'She's a wonderful cook and baker, better than me, for sure. She makes all the breakfast and lunch menu items, along with her now famous pastries, for the guests that stay at the vacation rental apartments, as well as any tourists that just come for lunch or breakfast while on one of the excursion packages. Heck, we even get locals coming up here to check out what we've done with this old place. The resort is a dream come true.'*

Just then, a man walked into the gift shop and snapped Ana out of her thoughts. "Good morning, sir. How may I help you?" asked Ana in English. One look at him and she knew he wasn't a native.

"I'm just looking, thanks," answered the man with an Irish accent. He was clearly not a local. He had flaming red hair and a neatly trimmed red mustache and beard, freckles on his face and arms, and piercing green eyes. He was in his late twenties, maybe early thirties, and had a rather rugged face. Red heads were a rarity on the island and Ana studied him intently.

"Are you a guest at the resort?" asked Ana. "If so, I can offer you a discount on any item in the gift shop."

"Umm, no. I'm just passing through," he said as he carefully examined each item on the shelves.

"Oh, so you came to see Friar's Cave, did you?" asked Ana, now curious about his mysterious behavior.

"Yes, yes, I came to see the cave. Is there a tour guide who can take me up to see it?" he asked. Now he was closely studying the art that hung on the walls.

"Oh, of course. I'll get someone to assist you," she said as she stepped out from behind the counter and headed toward the back office where the girls were.

"Rosana, there's a gentleman in the gift shop who wants a tour of the cave. Can you please go talk to him?" asked Ana.

"Sure," said Rosana as she headed toward the gift shop, followed by Ana. But when they got there, the shop was empty.

"That's strange," said Ana. "He was just here, but he didn't say much. He was pretty mysterious."

Rosana's stomach did a flip as the smile left her face. "What did he look like?" she asked.

Ana described the man. As she did, she felt a veil of dread descend upon her. She looked at Rosana and knew she felt the same way. *What if this man wasn't an innocent passerby but someone connected to the ordeal that took place four years ago?'* she thought.

"Could he be connected to the drug lord?" Ana asked. "If so, why is he coming back after four years? It doesn't make any sense."

Rosana didn't say anything. She was deep in thought trying to figure out if their lives would somehow be turned upside down again and prayed that it was just an innocent event unrelated to anything in the past.

"Don't worry about it, Mom," she said. "Let's get back to work." But secretly, she was worried.

When Rosana got back to the office, Angelo was there with an eager look on his face. "Oh good! I'm glad you're here. I would like to run something past you," he said with excitement in his voice and a big smile on his face. "I was preparing the dogs to go out hunting later when a man—I'm assuming he's a guest—started talking to me about the dogs. He asked why there were three dogs on the property. I told him they go hunting with me. He looked surprised and asked me if we offered hunting trips. I told him we didn't. So, then he asked me if he could accompany me on my hunt. I told him it was okay, but I started wondering, 'why don't we offer hunting trips?' There is no one on this island, or the nearby islands for that matter, who offers hunting trips. We have lots of game here such as peasants, wild boars, wolves, foxes, and other animals they could hunt. Why don't we offer a hunting excursion to attract people to our resort?" he said excitingly.

Milena and Mira's faces beamed with delight.

"What a wonderful idea," said Mira.

"Only you would think of something like that, Dad. That's a great idea! Don't you think so Rosana?" asked Milena.

Rosana, still deep in thought about the mysterious man, wasn't jumping for joy. "What did this man look like?" she asked.

Angelo was taken aback by her response, but answered her anyway. He described the red-headed man who approached him. Now Rosana was more concerned than ever. She told the three of them what just happened in the gift shop.

"Well, I highly doubt that there is any connection," said Angelo. "No one has bothered us in four years. Besides, they know we don't have the money nor the treasure. What could they possibly be after?" he innocently asked.

Milena and Rosana looked at each other as if a light bulb had turned on. They both realized that they did, in fact, still have something very valuable in their possession … the treasure map embossed on a silver sheet of paper! They never told anyone about it, not because they were trying to hide it from them. In reality, it simply slipped their minds as inconsequential in the big picture of everything that happened four years ago. Plus, the map wasn't in the cave, but in Steve's house so, they didn't even think to mention it. And in order not to alarm anyone any further Rosana decided to continue to keep it quiet, at least for now.

"Yes, you're right Angelo," Rosana said. "Silly me. I just overacted. I think your hunting idea is perfect. What about the liability insurance, though? We need to have insurance to protect ourselves against law suits should something happen to one of the hunters … and we need it for the dive experience too," she added looking at Milena.

"No worries," said Milena. "I can call our insurance agent and see what he says about increasing the coverage to include that. But, thank you for thinking of that. It totally slipped my mind," she said smiling and giving Rosana a quick hug.

"Great, it's settled then. I'll work on putting together a brochure that you gals can spruce up a bit," said Angelo as he walked out the door. With that, Mira left too, as she had her own chores to take care of in preparation for the day's activities.

Milena and Rosana were left alone in the office. They both sat down behind their desks, which faced each other, and began discussing the possibility of the mysterious man being part of their past.

"I thought all our fears were over years ago," said Rosana. "Now, I'm not so sure. What do you think we should do? Do you think we should talk to this man just to see where it goes?"

"Well, I don't know what else we can do. We can't just come out and ask him if he is connected in any way to a drug lord?" replied Milena. "My dad will probably engage him in conversation during the hunt today. Let's see what we can glean from their conversation first before we start speculating about something that may not even be a problem."

"You know how I am," said Rosana. "My Spidey senses tell me there is trouble ahead. I'm usually right."

"So, what do you propose we do?" asked Milena.

"I think we need to find a way to talk to him alone," came her reply. "But we need to figure out how to do that without sounding like we know something."

"I agree," Milena said. "Honestly, I couldn't stop thinking about that treasure map. I just didn't say anything because I knew you weren't ready to hear it. We found it taped to the bottom of one of Steve's dresser drawers, so you know he thought it was real too. That's a great hiding place."

"Yes, I was secretly hoping you'd forgotten about that," replied Rosana, dreading where this conversation was going.

"Why? Weren't you curious if there really is buried treasure on the Island of Iz?" asked Milena.

Iz was located west of Pasman in between Dugi Island (long island) and Pasman Island, in the Adriatic Sea.

"I think the map is authentic because it's hammered into a sheet made of silver," said Milena. "In ancient times, they did that to preserve important documents. The silver kept the document from disintegrating like paper documents would after a long time. Plus, pure silver and gold will never rust, as they don't contain iron while other metals do. Documents and maps on silver sheets don't disintegrate as easily as parchment paper either. So, that map has to be real. Why else is it printed on a silver sheet of paper?"

"Who do you think left the map?" asked Rosana nervously.

"No one from recent times. I think it was the Vikings. Many of the Knights Templars were Viking," said Milena. "But the map said 'Alaric's Treasure.' Do you know what that means?"

"I don't know much about King Alaric. I'll have to research it. But I do know that King Alaric died from illness and was buried with his treasure in what many believe is the Busento river in southern Italy. That's all I know. But, how do you think Steve got the map?" asked Rosana. "And how do you suppose the treasure found its way to Iz island?"

"I don't know. Maybe the map was already taped to the underside of the drawer when Steve bought the dresser," replied Milena. "Folks who move to Croatia typically go to Italy to buy their furniture. Steve sure was a mysterious man. I don't have any idea where he could have gotten the map. Heck, he didn't even tell us beforehand that he was leaving everything he owned to us, much less that he had a treasure map."

"Assuming that this red-headed man is here for the map, maybe he's the one who owned it before and the one who taped the map under the dresser drawer. Maybe somehow that chest of drawers was sold to Steve by accident and the red-headed man didn't know who actually bought it. And maybe Steve didn't even realize that a map was taped to the bottom of the drawer," replied Rosana.

"Oh, come on. Now you're saying Steve didn't know about the map, after all these years? What is the likelihood of that scenario? That's bizarre," said Milena with a slight chuckle.

"Why is that so strange? Look at all the stuff that happened four years ago. Don't you think it was strange that we found the Knights Templar treasure in a hidden vault, and that Mario found it too and hid the cocaine in there? What's so strange about some guy taping a map to the bottom of a drawer?" countered Rosana.

"If this red-headed guy did that, why would he have let the dresser out of his sight?" asked Milena.

"I don't know," said Rosana annoyingly, "maybe he was in jail or got drafted into the service or something... I don't know. Maybe he left it in his apartment that he shared with a roommate or maybe sub-leased it to someone who sold all his furniture while he was gone. I know it sounds far-fetched, but it's possible, and certainly stranger things have already happened. I have no idea how or why Steve wound up with it, but it's not out of the realm of possibility that it once belonged to this red-headed guy, whatever the circumstances were. And before you ask, no, I don't know how he tracked it down here after all these years," said Rosana. "Besides, Steve has lived on this island for a long time and no one came looking for the map. I'm guessing that all this publicity about the treasure put a bug up the red-head's ass and he is here on a whim."

"So, what are we going to do?" asked Milena.

"First, we need to find an opportunity to talk to him and get some information as to why he is here. It may all be innocent. But if we get the inkling that he's here for the treasure map, we have a problem," said Rosana.

— — —

Later that day, Angelo gathered the dogs and took the red-headed man on the hunt with him. Since the man didn't have his own gun, Angelo gave him a rifle to use. To secure the loan of the gun, he made a copy of the man's ID. Angelo had also packed a couple of sandwiches and some cold drinks into a small cooler, so they were ready to go hunting.

As they ascended the mountain, Angelo started a conversation with the man. He knew his name was Robert McCormick from his ID, at which time he introduced himself simply as Angelo. He figured the less Mr. McCormick knew about him and his relationship to the girls, the better.

They talked about the type of game that could be found on the island, and Mr. McCormick seemed friendly and easy enough to talk to. They were now on a first name basis. Robert told him that he never hunted before, but was always interested in it. He knew how to fire a rifle, but didn't have much practice. Angelo was feeling at ease with Robert and just about dismissed the idea that he had anything to do with the events of what happened four years ago. But, just as quickly, things began to change.

"Angelo, I heard that there was a treasure, Knights Templar treasure actually, that was found in the cave up on the mountain. Would you be able to take me there?" he asked.

"Sure, but don't you want to see if you could hunt something first?" answered Angelo, wondering why the man had a sudden change of interest.

"Well, I just wanted to see the cave. It shouldn't take long, right? Then we can continue with the hunt, if that's okay with you?" asked Robert.

Angelo thought it was a bit strange but decided to go along with Robert. He kept a wary eye on him now.

Angelo took Robert to the cave and showed him the friar statue and also explained how the statue was formed. But Robert started asking more questions.

"I heard there were a few murders up here. Can you tell me about that?" he asked.

"Uh … sure …" Angelo replied hesitantly. "I'm sure you know from reading the papers, two of our local cops shot a man in this cave, and there was a man who committed suicide here," said Angelo trying to keep things as vague as possible.

"Yes, I did read about that in the papers. The papers said that the Knights Templar treasure was discovered inside a hidden vault. Do you know where that vault is?" asked Robert.

"No, I don't. The cops wouldn't allow us inside the vault," he lied.

But Robert knew Angelo was lying. After looking around the cave for about fifteen minutes, Robert asked Angelo to take him back to hunting. Angelo got the feeling that Robert was playing it cool and was going to come back to the cave at a later time on his own. Now Angelo was worried that the past had come to haunt them again. He continued with the hunting trip, but after having no success, they decided to take a break and sat under an olive tree to eat their lunch.

"Angelo, what type of treasure did they find in the cave?" asked Robert.

"The antiquities experts from Zagreb found gold and silver coins, jewels, crowns, and some ancient artifacts. They took all of that to the museum where they conducted scientific tests to authenticate the discovery," said Angelo. "It was all done under strict security protocol. No one was allowed into the cave."

"But I read that two local girls found the treasure," said Robert.

"Actually, that's not completely true. It was the local man who was shot by the police who actually found the treasure, not the girls," said Angelo, trying to deflect attention away from the girls in an attempt to keep them out of danger.

"Oh really," said Robert. "I guess the media got it wrong, huh? The girls were hailed as heroines by the paper."

"No, they may have been hailed as heroines, but it was actually the local man who was the hero, not them."

"Oh, you mean Steve? The man who was shot by the cops?" asked Robert in feigned innocence. "Did they find anything else?"

"Not that I know of," said Angelo wondering what Robert was getting at.

"Well, you know, sometimes pirates also hide treasure maps along with their loot," elaborated Robert, hoping to get more information out of Angelo without actually telling him what he was looking for.

"Nope, not that I know of," answered Angelo. "The antiquities dealers took everything with them back to Zagreb."

"So, what type of stuff did the cops steal?" Robert kept prodding.

"From what I understand, they took some of the gold coins and some of the jewelry," said Angelo. "But as you know, they were killed in Venezuela. By the way, Robert, what do you do for a living? It sounds like you're going to write a book. Is that what you do? Are you a writer?"

"I do some blogging, but I don't write books," came Robert's quick reply.

"Oh, so you're going to blog about the treasure … four years later?" asked Angelo immediately wishing he could retract the question.

"No, not just the treasure, but also about the people and town and how the events have changed everyone's lives," he said, trying to come up with a good story on the fly.

But Angelo's mind was already made up. Robert, if that was even his real name, was lying. Angelo knew the man was fishing for clues for something. He worried for the girls and wanted to get back to the resort as quickly as possible. "Yes, that's right," said Angelo. "The entire town hailed Steve for his heroic attempts to stop the rogue cops from stealing the treasure."

The two men sat in silence as they finished their lunch. But Angelo's stomach was in knots. He needed to get back to the girls to tell them what had happened. Now it was Angelo's turn to feign innocence. "I don't know about you, but I'm getting tired. I think I've had enough hunting for one day. Where are you staying? Will you want to go on another hunt?" he asked, hoping Robert would say 'no' to the hunting trip question.

"I'm staying at a hotel in Ugljan," said Robert. "I'll phone ahead when my friends and I are ready for a hunting trip."

'*Umm,*' thought Angelo, '*when his friends are ready? Why aren't his friends here now with him on this hunting trip? I don't like this and I think there's more to this man than meets the eye. This sounds fishy and I'm worried about the girls. I thought the events of four years ago were over, but now, I'm not so sure. God, I hope it's over and this is just an innocent event, but somehow, I don't think so.*'

They made their way back to the resort in silence. Once they arrived, Robert returned the gun he borrowed and the two men said their goodbyes and parted ways. Angelo put the dogs back into their gated area and immediately went to find the girls. They were in the office, so Angelo stepped inside and closed the door behind him.

"I need to talk to you," he said with furled eyebrows.

"What's wrong, Dad?" asked Milena.

"Remember the red-headed man who came to the gift shop? I took him hunting with me. It was obvious to me that he was fishing for information, but I don't know exactly what he was after," said Angelo. He told the girls the conversations he had with Robert and told them he was concerned for their safety. "Why would he be interested in writing a blog about events that happened four years ago? That's a long time to wait," said Angelo.

"Dad, there's something we didn't tell you. So, I might as well tell you now," said Milena a bit hesitantly. "When we were cleaning Steve's place, we found a treasure map. The map was embossed on a piece of silver paper. Rosana and I think that's what he was looking for."

"Why didn't you say anything sooner?" asked Angelo trying hard not to lose his patience with both girls over this.

"With all the commotion, it actually slipped our minds. And then when we did think of it, we didn't want to tell you because we didn't want to worry you anymore than we had worried you already. I'm sorry, Dad," apologized Milena.

"So, what are you going to do with the map?" asked Angelo. Both girls were silent. But Angelo could tell by the looks on their faces that they already had a plan. "Seriously? You're going to endanger yourselves all over again? Are you crazy?!" asked Angelo, now unable to keep calm.

"Dad, we aren't putting our lives in danger. No one knows about the map, except maybe this Robert guy. Rosana and I figured it must be a real map. After all, no one would emboss a fake map on silver paper. But if Robert does know about the map, then he just confirmed to us that the map is real. And remember, we know Iz island a lot better than he does. Plus, I am going to talk to Goran. Our plan is to go to Iz, with Goran for protection, and find the treasure ourselves."

"I still think you're both being reckless!" said Angelo.

"Angelo, please come and help me with this box," Mira called out, which distracted Angelo. He shook his head and let out a deep sigh as he left to go help his wife.

Rosana was very quiet until then, and then she spoke up.

"Milena, we have our hands full here running our business. We can't afford to go off chasing some fabled treasure. Yes, we think the map is real, but it's based on the fabled story of King Alaric. We just don't have the time to go off digging for treasure that may or may not be there."

"Rosana, that's why it's called a treasure hunt," she said smiling. "We have enough money already with what Steve left us, and our business is generating a good income. So, we can afford to take some time off. We can hire a general manager to oversee the businesses. Come on, Rosana. Aren't you up for another adventure? It will be fun," she pleaded.

Rosana thought back on the adventures they had in finding the Knights Templar treasure and all the events that led up to it. It was all very rewarding and Milena's offer was very tempting, but she still had her reservations. *'Look what happened to Steve and Butch,'* she reminded herself. *'And what about all the other people who died? And being taken hostage? And the vengeful drug lords? Do I really want to risk going through that type of danger and stress again?'*

She remembered that there were times when she thought she was going to die, and she remembered very well that she had a weak heart that, at times, beat wildly in her chest. She didn't enjoy feeling that way. It was too stressful for her, and she thought at times her heart would burst. She knew she had to put her health first and foremost. But she also knew she couldn't fight the adventurous spirit running through her veins. She knew that eventually she'd get bored with running the resort, though, right now running the business did pump up her adrenaline.

'I'll go see a doctor about my heart. Maybe if I take medication for AFib, my heart won't be so much of a problem,' she thought. *'What should I do?'* She looked over and saw Milena watching her with bated breath, and waiting for an answer.

Rosana looked at Milena and gave her a big smile.

"SURE!" she said as she extended her hand to shake Milena's, as if to seal the agreement. "After all, don't they say that 'happiness is having something to look forward to?'"

-The End-

ACKNOWLEDGMENTS

My gratitude and love to:

My alter ego, Biserka Bacić, who told me about the naturally formed friar's statue in the Friar's Cave located on the island of Pasman in Croatia. Thank you for sparking my imagination to write a fictional story where the cave becomes one of the main characters.

My beautiful and talented daughter, Dawn Josephson, for your invaluable guidance through the writing and publishing process.

My husband and my rock, Frederick Husher, for your support and patience during the process.

ABOUT THE AUTHOR

Sylvia Bigit's latest book, *The Friar Cave Mysteries*, is an action and adventure mystery fiction that takes place on a paradise island off the Dalmatian coast of Croatia. Her first book, *Escape From Tyranny: Through a Child's Eyes*, is a memoir of her early childhood living in communist Yugoslavia. She has also written numerous business articles, press releases, Wikipedia pages, technical user software manuals, and other business-related documents. Prior to writing her books, Sylvia held positions such as VP of Operations, Director of IT Services, Business Manager, Systems Analyst, Business Analyst and Corporate Communications Writer.

Sylvia has a passion for world culture and has traveled extensively to many parts of the world both for business and pleasure. She now lives in the sunshine state of Florida.